THE
SLICK-IRON
TRAIL

Center Point
Large Print

Also by Bradford Scott and available from Center Point Large Print:

Gunsmoke on the Rio Grande
The Hate Trail
Lone Star Rider

THE SLICK-IRON TRAIL

Bradford Scott

CENTER POINT LARGE PRINT
THORNDIKE, MAINE

This Center Point Large Print edition is published
in the year 2016 by arrangement with
Golden West Literary Agency.

First US edition: Arcadia House.

The text of this Large Print edition is unabridged.
In other aspects, this book may vary
from the original edition.
Printed in the United States of America
on permanent paper.
Set in 16-point Times New Roman type.

ISBN: 978-1-68324-148-5 (hardcover)
ISBN: 978-1-68324-152-2 (paperback)

Library of Congress Cataloging-in-Publication Data

Names: Scott, Bradford, 1893–1975, author.
Title: The slick-iron trail / Bradford Scott.
Description: Center Point Large Print edition. | Thorndike, Maine :
Center Point Large Print, 2016.
Identifiers: LCCN 2016030047| ISBN 9781683241485 (hardcover :
alk. paper) | ISBN 9781683241522 (pbk. : alk. paper)
Subjects: LCSH: Large type books. | GSAFD: Western stories.
Classification: LCC PS3537.C9265 S63 2016 | DDC 813/.52—dc23
LC record available at https://lccn.loc.gov/2016030047

THE
SLICK-IRON
TRAIL

Chapter One

"Shadow, if the Good Lord ever made anything more beautiful, I figure He must have kept it for Himself!"

Sitting his great black horse on the crest of a tall ridge, Ranger Walt Slade, named by the peons of the Rio Grande river *El Halcon*—The Hawk— gazed with appreciative eyes at the stupendous panorama spread before him.

Towering, many-colored, misty and unreal, the Chisos Mountains bulked against the southwest horizon, a bewildering kaleidoscope of unbelievable color—blue, red, purple and yellow—their vivid tints surpassed in impressiveness only by their austere ruggedness. Farther to the south the scene was appallingly desolate, but weirdly lovely. The gray-green of the sage was dotted with the more vivid hues of prickly pear, yucca and octillo. Beyond the middle distance a streak of blazing white gleamed like an earthbound Milky Way spangled and jeweled in the early morning sunlight—the salt-encrusted shore of a salt lake that lay like the bleached bones of a dead hand awaiting burial.

Closer to hand rose sheer mountain walls of vivid purple and misty violet. Far to the southeast

7

rose the Carmen Mountains of Mexico, a deep velvety red in the sun-glow, which would fade to a sultry maroon when the level light poured from low in the west to beat upon their mighty battlements like golden sword strokes on sable armor.

Between the frozen rainbow of the Chisos and the gold-splashed ruby pool of the Carmens, to the east and the west, is a land where ranching was and is supreme. It is an unbelievable land of legend and tradition, of outlandish deeds, of romance and fantastic adventure that are but part of the day's work. Men bulk big in this land where men are few. They absorb the qualities of the land of distances and desolation in which they live.

Cattle in the Texas Big Bend country require vast acreages; the only grassy ranges are in mountain valleys. But uncrowded conditions and the climate produce healthy animals of unusually high quality. The grasses and the curly mesquite have in them enough of the distilled spirit of the vast sun and the sweet rain of the dry country to plump out a gaunt steer into a fat and frisky beef in a month's grazing.

Walt Slade knew all this, and there was a pleased expression on his high-nosed, sternly handsome face as he rode down the opposite slope, following a trail that wound on with many a bend and chaparral-shrouded turn through a narrow valley which wended north by east.

Slade and Shadow heard it at about the same time, a rhythmic clicking bearing down from the north—the beat of fast hoofs on the stony ground. Shadow's ears pricked forward, and Slade became a trifle more alert.

Around a bend bulged a band of hard-riding horsemen, eight in number. Foremost was a broad-shouldered, deep-chested man with abnormally long arms. He had a round, ruddy and good-humored face dominated by snapping dark eyes. His black hair was crisp and curly, his mouth wide and firm. He wore regulation range garb and forked his big bay with the careless grace of a lifetime in the saddle. Slade noted that he carried two guns and that a rifle butt projected from the saddle boot under his left thigh. His followers were salty-looking hombres of assorted size and build with nothing particularly outstanding about any of them.

The bunch pulled to a halt at sight of Slade and sat their horses, tense and watchful, as he drew near. The big man waved a hand.

"Howdy, cowboy?" he called in a jovial voice. "See anything of a bunch of scalawags shoving a herd of cows down this way, fast?"

"I cut into this trail from the west just a couple of miles back," Slade replied as Shadow ambled to a standstill. "Haven't met anybody headed south."

The other nodded. "Reckon they were at the forks ahead of you, then," he replied. "They ought to be an hour or so ahead of us. Come on, boys; hightail. We'll catch 'em yet."

Suddenly he fixed his glittering gaze on Slade's face. "And you didn't meet anybody on the west trail?"

Slade shook his head.

"Ride it quite a piece?" the other persisted.

"A good many miles," Slade answered.

The other nodded again and gathered up his reins. "Sure about it, eh?"

This time El Halcon's only reply was a nod.

"Then they sure must have headed on south to the river," the big man said. "*Adios.* See you in town when we get back, if you're headed that way. Sorry to have pestered you, but there's more cows in that wide-looped bunch than I can afford to lose. *Adios*!"

With his grimly silent bunch pounding after him, he swept past Slade with another friendly wave of his hand and vanished around the next bulge.

Slade gazed speculatively at the settling cloud of dust which marked the passing of the group.

"Well, that was about as salty a straggling as I ever looked at," he observed to Shadow. "Reckon the jiggers they're after are in for a lively time if they catch up with them. In my opinion, however, they're following a cold trail; that is, unless the bunch in front took a short cut up ahead somewhere. Plenty of cows have passed this way, all right, but I'm ready to bet a hatful of pesos that none have come along during the past twenty-four hours. This section is a network of snake tracks, though, lots of them so old nobody knows who first rode them. They could have turned off somewhere. Most of the trails head for the Comanche Crossing, however, and I reckon the bunch following the cows know what they're about and where to head off the slick ironers. Let's go, horse. We've got to find a place to cook something to eat and knock off a little shut-eye. After two nights and a day in the hull, I'm beginning to feel a mite peaked."

The trail left the valley and climbed into the hills, poured through a notch and wound along the edge of a dizzy precipice that walled a narrow canyon which, Slade could see, turned sharply to the west and bored its way through the range for an indeterminate distance. The floor of the gorge was heavily brush-grown, with a swift stream of dark water washing the base of the near wall perhaps fifty feet below the surface of the trail.

Slade had ridden for perhaps half an hour, with the precipice on one side and the craggy mountain wall on the other, when again he heard the beat of fast hoofs drawing toward him. Another moment, and around a bend swept a second hard-riding group.

"What in blazes!" he muttered. "Has a cage busted somewhere?"

The second group, about equal in number to the first, was headed by a lanky, cold-eyed old man with a drooping mustache. A silver shield gleamed on his shirt front and bore the legend, "Sheriff," embossed on its surface in gold.

Riding stirrup to stirrup with the sheriff was a tall, well-formed man with a somewhat swarthy, straight-featured face and keen brown eyes. Jostling behind the pair were half a dozen men garbed as cowhands.

The group pulled to a slithering halt and eyed the approaching horseman. Slade pulled up within a dozen feet of them and returned their gaze.

"Where'd you come from, cowboy?" the sheriff asked in harsh tones, eyeing Slade with scant favor.

"I don't ask you where you came from," El Halcon drawled the easy reply.

The sheriff stiffened, apparently started to make a tart rejoinder, then evidently changed his mind.

"Reckon the question was out of order," he admitted. "I was figuring maybe you noted a bunch of hellions skalleyhooting south."

"Can't say for sure," Slade returned, "but I did meet some salty-looking gents, one of whom said they were on the trail of a bunch that had lifted some of their cows."

The sheriff's eyes widened; he seemed to

breathe with difficulty. "Just what did that talkin' hellion look like?" he asked.

Slade described the jovial, curly-haired man. The sheriff let loose an appalling flood of profanity. Slade listened admiringly.

"Curly Bill Elkins, that blankety-blank!" bawled the sheriff. "Trailing wide-looped cows! The nerve of that ring-tailed sidewinder! Let me line sights with him just once!"

Slade's eyes had narrowed the merest trifle as the sheriff pronounced the name, but he merely asked mildly:

"Fellow done something wrong?"

The sheriff seemed on the verge of apoplexy. "You trying to be funny?" he bellowed.

Slade struggled with a grin. The sheriff's followers also appeared to be afflicted by some emotion that reddened their faces and brightened their eyes.

"I was just asking for information," Slade replied, his voice serious but his eyes dancing. The sheriff's rage *did* have a mirth-provoking side.

"If holding up a stagecoach and killing the driver is wrong, he did," the sheriff informed him, his voice ominously quiet. "You say that outfit was headed south?"

All the laughter left Slade's eyes, and they were abruptly as serious as his voice. He gave, in precise detail, an account of his meeting with the group. The sheriff nodded, appeared to consider. He looked Slade up and down.

"It's a wonder they didn't do for you," he said, "seeing as they'd know you'd meet us and give us the lowdown on which way they were headed." His gaze rested on the heavy guns flaring out from El Halcon's sinewy hips, shifted to his slim, quiet, capable-looking hands that seemed never far away from the plain black butts of the guns.

"Reckon they would have if they hadn't figured it would be considerable of a chore and one they wouldn't particularly enjoy before they finished with it," he said. "And they were headed south, you say? Well, this is where I drop a loop on that hellion once and for all."

The tall, good-looking man on the sheriff's right spoke for the first time.

"*If* you find the loot on him," he said with significant emphasis. "Otherwise it will be the same old story and he'll slide out of your loop. Nobody has ever been able to pin anything on Curly Bill Elkins. Remember, the bunch that held up the stage were masked, and the wounded messenger they left for dead admitted he couldn't identify any faces."

"He'll have the stuff on him, all right," declared the sheriff. "Right now he's headed for Mexico to trade it in for dobe dollars that can't be identified. But the Crossing will hold him up, the shape the river is in now. We'll get him. You're sure they were headed south?" he repeated to Slade.

"That's right; when I met them," Slade replied.

"Mighty apt to stick to the main Yucca Trail, then," commented the sheriff. "It's the straight road to the Crossing."

Suddenly Slade recalled the last question the curly-haired man had shot at him.

"They seemed interested in the trail to the west," he told the sheriff. "Asked me a couple of times if I'd met anybody on it."

"They wouldn't turn off that way," the sheriff declared with conviction. "They'll keep on south to the river and the ford. Come on, boys."

"Just a minute, Blevins," the tall man interrupted. "Fellow," he said to Slade, "could you repeat carefully just how the hellion worded what he said?"

Slade did, so far as he recalled. The other nodded thoughtfully, but the sheriff snorted with impatience.

"Oh, come along, Girton," he said. "We're wasting time. Thanks for what you told us, feller; it may be a help," he added with a nod to Slade. "Let's go!"

The posse rode on, swiftly gathering speed. Slade shook his black head and continued on his way.

"Well, horse," he observed to Shadow, "looks like we barged smack into the jigger we were sent over here to investigate and didn't know

15

him from Adam, although he was dressed sort of different. And the sheriff figures he had just robbed a stage and killed the driver. Wonder if he did turn west, or if what he said was just a cute little trick, because he figured I'd pass the word to the sheriff when I met him. Well, if it was, I fell for it. I'd like to amble along after the sheriff, but you're in no shape for a hard ride to the Rio Grande, and neither am I. Horse, I'm getting plumb woozy."

Slade wasn't in very good shape and he knew it. Nearly forty-eight sleepless hours, most of them in the saddle, were beginning to take their toll. His eyes refused to focus correctly, and he was deathly tired. He heaved a sigh of relief as the trail dropped into another valley and a welcome gleam appeared about a mile to the left. Turning the big black, he made for the water, a small stream that hugged the steep valley wall. Pulling up in the shade of a bristle of growth, he got the rig off Shadow and turned him loose to graze. Very quickly he had a fire going, bacon and a couple of eggs sizzling in a small skillet and coffee bubbling in a little flat bucket. He ate his simple meal and felt considerably better. Then, after smoking a cigarette, he curled up on his blanket and was almost instantly asleep.

Chapter Two

When Slade awoke, he knew he had slept for hours. The sun was low in the west, the shadows lengthening. Greatly refreshed, he boiled what was left of the coffee and swallowed several satisfying cups.

"But that scrapes the bottom of the barrel," he told Shadow. "My pouches are plumb empty. Well, we shouldn't be many hours from Chino, the town we're heading for. So let's go, horse; I've got a notion you could stand a helping of oats after living on grass for quite a spell. Wonder if the sheriff had any luck. Either way he should have headed back in this direction long ago, unless he followed those jiggers across the river into Mexico, which isn't likely. Let's go!"

The sun sank in scarlet and gold behind the western crags. Purple shadows brimmed the canyon along the edge of which the trail now ran. The cliff tops glowed briefly with reflected light, then dimmed and grayed, and the world was swallowed up in darkness.

But not for long. A half-moon slid from behind a cloud bank in the west, tipped the crests with frosty silver and flooded the rugged scene with

17

ghostly radiance. Slade rode on through the wild and weird beauty of the night.

The moon was dropping down the sky when the hills fell away, Slade rode through the jaws of a narrow pass and saw a wide valley walled by towering slopes misty in the distance. The Yucca Trail dipped sharply downward, followed a long slope that leveled off to the valley floor some two miles distant. Perhaps three miles farther on, he could make out a cluster of winking sparks that doubtless marked the site of the cow and mining town of Chino for which he was heading.

"Stir the dust, horse," he told Shadow, "or we'll be late for supper." Shadow snorted in response and quickened his pace.

They reached the valley floor, where the trail wound between clumps of growth and some groves. The stream cutting across the range was very likely the one that flowed through the canyon so turbulently some miles to the south. Fine pasture, all right, Slade decided. Grass that was belly high on a horse, and apparently plenty of water.

A mile from where the trail reached the valley floor they passed through a wide grove, where the shadows lay black and solid beneath the trees. A final straggle of growth, and Slade pulled up and gazed across the rolling rangeland at a big, imposing-looking house built in a heavy Spanish style.

With a cattleman's appreciation, he surveyed the tight barns, commodious bunkhouse and other buildings that flanked the great *casa*. The hombre who squatted there must be pretty well heeled with dinero, he concluded. As he drew nearer, he noted that, although in excellent repair, the buildings were undoubtedly old.

Passing the ranchhouse, he rode across fertile rangeland upon which grazed plenty of fat cows. Slade was able to decipher the brand on some of them, a rather unusual brand, a sprawling S running longitudinally. Snake S, Slade defined it.

The valley, he estimated, was some forty miles long by perhaps twenty-five in width, one of the unexpected great "oasis" regions encountered frequently in the heart of the wild desert and mountain country of the Big Bend.

The cluster of lights ahead resolved into a huddle of buildings covering a considerable acreage. As he approached the town, Slade was conscious of a monotonous pound and grumble. Stamp mills, big ones, ground the ore brought from the mines in the hills to a watery paste from which the precious metal would be extracted by the amalgam process. In addition to its thriving cattle business, Chino acquired profit from the mines for which it was a supply depot and shipping center. No wonder outlaw bands were harassing the section. Rich picking was to be had by enterprising gents of easy conscience. Slade wondered if Curly Bill Elkins, elusive and wily, really was the head of the outlaw faction, as reports coming to the Ranger Post headquarters insisted he was. But if he was, so far nobody had been able to pin anything on Elkins, who, no matter what he had been south of the Rio Grande, now posed as a respectable rancher. Well, it was up to him, Slade, to find out—that was what he was here for.

Soon Slade found himself riding through the straggling outskirts of the town. He passed along a shadowy side street and could hear the hum of Chino's busy main thoroughfare immediately ahead.

Abruptly he heard something else—a crackle of shots, a wild yelling and a pound of approaching hoofs. He quickened Shadow's pace and a moment later reached a place where the side street turned into another that was wider and much better lighted.

Up the street, whooping and yelling, rode three horsemen. A taut rope stretched from the saddle horn of the last rider. The far end of the rope was looped around the body of a man who bounded forward frantically to keep from being jerked off his feet.

Even as Slade stared at the unusual sight, the victim lost his footing and pitched headlong into the dust. Instantly the rope tightened. A series of piercing howls arose, and the unfortunate was dragged through the dust and over the ruts. The horsemen swept past the mouth of the side street, whooping exultantly.

Walt Slade's right hand flashed down and up. There was a spurt of fire, the sullen boom of his heavy Colt. The victim, his painful progress abruptly interrupted, sprawled in the street, screeching with pain and fright. Over him tangled the coils of the rope severed by Slade's bullet.

The three horsemen, with shouts of anger, whirled their mounts "on a dime" to face Slade. Their hands dropped. Then they stiffened, tense and motionless. They were staring into the muzzles, one wisping smoke, of two long black guns. And back of those unwavering gun muzzles was the towering form of El Halcon.

Slade broke the silence. "What's the notion?" he called harshly. "Want to kill that jigger?"

A chorus of angry shouts answered him as the horsemen yelled incoherently in their anger.

"What the blazes do you mean by horning in on something that don't concern you?" demanded a wiry, sandy-haired individual whose face bore a red welt, seared there by the backlash of the severed rope that still dangled from his saddle horn.

"Reckon such carryings-on are anybody's concern," Slade replied quietly. "Three men jumping on one isn't very creditable, to my way of thinking. I ask you again, what's the notion?"

The cowboys flushed under the searing contempt in Slade's voice, but still were not subdued.

"He's one of the blasted Peralta outfit, and he was told to stay out of town!" bawled a beefy, fat-faced cowboy who rode next to the sandy-haired man. "And if you didn't have the drop on us, I'd—*yowp!*"

The threat ended in a yelp of alarm as Slade's hands moved with flickering speed; but only to slide the big guns back in their sheaths. Empty-handed, he faced the three horsemen.

"Haven't got the drop on you now," he observed pointedly, his voice silkily soft but edged with a steely threat.

The fat cowboy stared, his eyes blinking, his mouth hanging ajar. He opened and closed his hands nervously, glanced sideways at his companions. It was the sandy-haired man who broke the tension.

"Lay off, Bounce," he advised his companion. "You'd have about as much chance with this gent as a terrapin climbing a slick log.

"Maybe we were going a mite strong," he added, turning to Slade, "but that saddle-colored hellion was warned. We didn't aim to kill him; just figured to drag him out of town and turn him loose."

The victim of the attack had meanwhile freed himself from the rope and struggled to his feet. He was scratched and bleeding, but otherwise appeared little the worse for his experience. Now, his black eyes sparkling with rage and hate, he burst into a torrent of Spanish invective directed at his tormentors.

"Cinch up," Slade advised him. "You aren't damaged much, and swearing won't help matters."

But the other was not easily appeased. He shook his fist at the three horsemen.

"Why you no draw the gun now?" he taunted in imperfect English. "Why you no draw the gun on El Halcon?"

The speaker forgotten, the three cowboys stared at Slade.

"Whe-e-ew!" whistled the sandy-haired man. "And I was figuring on taking a chance and reachin'!"

The fat puncher shook his bristly head. "I'd have took a chance, if a hunk of dust hadn't got in my eye just then," he mumbled.

"Uh-huh," snorted the sandy-haired cowboy, "and then you'd have had dust in both eyes, only you wouldn't have noticed it. El Halcon! Feller, are you really El Halcon?"

"Been called that," Slade admitted. An amused light in his gray eyes, he fished the makings from his shirt pocket and rolled a cigarette with the slim fingers of his left hand. From the tail of his eye he noted the battered Mexican slide across the street and disappear into a dark opening between two buildings.

The three cowboys were meanwhile regarding

Slade with lively interest, shaking their heads and mumbling. The sandy-haired man spoke.

"Feller," he said, "my name's Price—Walsh Price. The jigger packing the tallow and the big-medicine mouth is Bounce Perkins. The talkative gent the other side of me is Tom Ord. We ride for old Rance Rutledge who owns the Tumbling R, the best spread in the section. Not quite as big as Steve Girton's Snake S, but even better grass."

Slade smiled acknowledgment. "Reckon you know my handle, eh?" he remarked.

"Uh-huh, we know it—who in Texas don't?" the other admitted.

"A slight exaggeration, I'd say," Slade replied.

"Ain't so sure about that," declared Price. "But anyhow, you look like a regular feller, despite the things we've heard about you. Glad to know you, Slade."

El Halcon smiled again, taking the somewhat dubious compliment as it was meant.

Price suddenly glanced about with an apprehensive air. "Sheriff Blevins is around somewhere, and if he heard the shooting he'll be over here rarin' and chargin'. And old Lake is a cold proposition, and in a mighty bad temper from having no luck chasin' Curly Bill Elkins and his hellions or some other sidewinders who robbed the Chino-Marlin stage. Think he's up at the stamp mills, though, and maybe didn't hear it. Anyhow, we were just figuring to stop off at the

Headlight saloon for a bite to eat when we got to arguing with that Mexican. If you'd like to join us—"

"That's the best thing I've heard you say yet," Slade applauded. "And how about a seat for my horse?"

"A horse like that's got a right to be served at any table," said Price, "but there's a good stable right around the corner where I expect he'll be more comfortable; we leave our cayuses there. Come along; we'll point the way. Say! What became of that Mexican?"

"Slid out of sight a minute ago," Slade replied. "Reckon he figured some place else was better than here."

"He figured right," grunted Price. "Not that we've got anything against Mexicans as Mexicans," he hastened to add. "Lots of 'em are first-rate jiggers. Why Steve Girton is half Mexican, real old Spanish blood, and there never was a finer feller than Steve. But that hellion is one of the Peralta outfit!"

A muttered oath finished the observation. Slade glanced inquiringly at the speaker, but Price did not see fit to amplify his remarks.

Chapter Three

The stable proved satisfactory. Right across the street was a small rooming house patronized by cowmen, where Slade obtained sleeping quarters and deposited his saddle pouches, rifle and other gear. Then, in company of Price and his companions, he repaired to the Headlight, which proved to be a big combination saloon and eating house. The group found a table and gave their orders.

"Uh-huh, it's fine rangeland," Price answered a question from Slade. "I figure there's no better cattle country in Texas than what the Big Bend provides in spots. This valley is one of 'em, and one of the best. Most folks who live here have been here a long time. There's several good-paying mines in the hills over east, too. Uh-huh, a fine section, or used to be. But one rotten apple can spoil a whole barrel."

Slade raised his eyes to the cowboy, but Price was glooming into his glass and said nothing more. His companions also had abruptly become morose. Slade rolled a cigarette and waited for them to break the silence.

Suddenly the swinging doors banged open and a man strode into the room, glancing keenly about.

With hardly an instant's hesitation he headed for the table occupied by Slade and his companions. Slade got an impression of steely slenderness topped by wide shoulders and a deep chest, the slenderness of a finely tempered rapier blade.

The man's face was also arresting. It was cameo-like in the regularity of its features, which were set off by flashing blue eyes and tawny hair. At the moment the fine-featured face was set in hard lines of vindictive anger that tightened the rather full lips and brought a touch of color to the ordinarily somewhat swarthy complexion. In height he was slightly more than six feet, with long arms and powerful-looking hands. He was dressed in somber black, relieved only by the snow of his ruffled shirt front. At his hip swung a heavy gun.

Within arm's length of the table the newcomer paused, glaring at its occupants. His voice rang out, hard, metallic, singularly clear and penetrating.

"Price," he said, "I told you once before about making trouble for my hands."

There was an implied threat in the statement, a threat that acted on the sandy-haired cowboy like a goad on a bull. With a roar of rage, he surged to his feet.

"Blast you, Peralta!" he bellowed. "I'll—"

Peralta hit him with both hands, hard. Price was fairly lifted off his feet. He crashed into the table and went over it with a crackle and bang of smashed crockery.

Walt Slade, sliding from his chair in a lithe ripple of motion, alone escaped the universal ruin. Bounce Perkins was flat on his back, a bowl of stew gumming his bristly hair. Bill Ord, drenched with steaming coffee, was on his hands and knees, floundering about like a disjointed frog. Price, partially dazed by the terrific punch he had taken on the jaw, flopped and writhed, trying to coordinate his numbed muscles.

Perkins and Ord came to their feet yelling curses. Peralta leaped forward, swinging with both hands. Perkins caught one squarely in the mouth, and his falling body smashed what was left of the table into kindling wood. Ord got in one blow that staggered Peralta, then took a long left on the cheek bone and landed beside Perkins.

Walsh Price managed to sit up. He seized a heavy bowl and hurled it at Peralta. It carromed off his shoulder and grazed his jaw, starting a trickle of blood. Peralta swore viciously, and his hand flashed down and up. The black muzzle of his gun lined with Price's breast. But just as he pulled trigger, Walt Slade's fingers coiled around his wrist like flexible rods of nickel steel, jerking the gun barrel aside.

The bullet fanned Price's face with its lethal breath. Peralta gave a yell of pain as Slade's grip ground his wrist bones together. The gun fell from his numbed hand and thudded on the floor. Writhing about, he swung a vicious blow at Slade's face.

Before it had traveled six inches it was blocked. At the same instant, a blow like a sledge-hammer smacked against Peralta's jaw with the sound of a butcher's cleaver slamming a side of beef. Slade let go of his wrist, and Peralta shot through the air and thudded to the floor. Slade's eye caught a gleam of steel on the far side of the room and went sideways and down. A long knife buzzed through the air and thudded against the wall to stand quivering and shimmering in the boards.

Slade drew in a flicker of movement and shot from the hip. The knife thrower, a thick-set, swarthy man, who had drawn a gun with his left hand, went reeling back, clutching at his blood-spouting arm. As Slade's barrel lined with him a second time he whirled about, plunged through a back door and vanished.

Bounce Perkins, spitting blood, teeth and curses, scrambled to his feet gripping a table leg. With a sputtering howl, he leaped toward the prostrate form of Peralta, whirling up his clubbed weapon. But Slade surged erect at that instant, the point of his shoulder caught Perkins in the chest, and Bounce sat down again, hard.

"Stay where you are while you're still able to sit up," Slade told him. A gun in each hand, he swept the room with their muzzles.

However, nobody else appeared to be looking for trouble. Men were under tables, crouched behind posts, hugging the wall. The long bar was astonishingly empty. From the bartenders squatted beneath its protection came muffled yells of "Stop it!"

Peralta sat up, looking dazed. He cast a wondering glance at Slade, shook his head as if in disbelief, and got slowly to his feet. All the fight in him had apparently evaporated. Slade slanted a glance at the disheveled Tumbling R cowboys, who were also standing up and looking as if they, too, had had a bellyful.

"I don't know what this is all about," the Ranger said, "but I figure it's gone far enough. Peralta—that's your name, I believe—get the blazes out of here. Price, you and the boys mosey over to that table by the wall and mop up. Tell the waiter to bring us something more to eat. All right, get going, all of you!"

Peralta gave him a long stare and shrugged his shoulders. He picked up his fallen gun, which he jammed into its holster, turned on his heel and walked rather unsteadily to the door. In the opening, he paused a moment, favored Slade with another stare, which was intensely speculative, and vanished. The Tumbling R punchers slouched over to the designated table and sat down. Men sidled back to the bar or their games. The bartenders bobbed into view like jacks-in-a-box.

Slade holstered his guns and joined the cowboys at the table. He alone bore no marks of conflict. He chuckled as he surveyed his companions.

Bounce Perkins had a badly cut mouth and was minus two teeth. Tom Ord had a black eye and a swelling nose. Price boasted a lump the size of an egg on the side of his jaw. He grimaced with pain as he essayed speech.

"Well," he said with the ghost of a grin, "no matter what you say about that yaller-haired horned toad, he's a fighting man! Oh, Lord! Here comes the sheriff!"

The old peace officer came in like a miniature cyclone; not so miniature, at that. He glared about and stormed over to the table. Pausing, he shook his fist at the battered cowboys.

"Explain yourselves!" he bellowed. "What's the notion—bustin' up the furniture and shootin' holes in the wall? Explain yourselves, I say, before I lock you up and throw the key away!"

"We didn't do nothin', Lake," Price protested. "We were just settin' down to eat when Manuel Peralta bulged in and landed on us like forty hen hawks on a settin' quail. Look at Bounce's teeth, and Ord's eye, and my jaw!"

"He'd oughta have shoved a boot down your blasted neck to shut you up!" declared the wrathful lawman. "And I suppose you didn't do anything to start Peralta off! Oh, no! Of course

31

not! You wouldn't think of such a thing! Which one of you took a shot at him?"

"Nobody took a shot at him," answered Price. "A saddle-colored hellion across the room flung a knife at Slade here, and Slade plugged him in the arm. That's what the shooting was about."

Sheriff Blevins whirled on Slade. "And you!" he bawled. "Why the blinkin' blue blazing blankety blank did *you* have to show up here? Haven't I got enough trouble with that infernal Bill Elkins and his sort without another of the same kind squatting here? I've a notion to throw you in the calaboose right now!"

"On what charge?" Slade asked cheerfully.

"Being a general darn nuisance would do as good as any," the sheriff retorted. "Oh, I know, nobody has ever been able to tie you up with anything, any more than they've been able to drop a loop on Elkins, but one thing is sure for certain; wherever you are, trouble sprouts like a toad-stool in the dark. Before you're in town an hour, there's a riot!"

"I wasn't looking for any riots," Slade complained.

"No, of course not!" snorted the sheriff. "But right away you're mixed up in one."

Slade deftly changed the subject and increased the sheriff's fury.

"Have any luck with your stage robbers?" he asked.

"No!" stormed the sheriff. "And you know blasted well I didn't. How about that bum steer you gave me about them taking the west fork of the trail?"

"I didn't say they took the west fork," Slade replied. "I just said they asked me questions about it.

"But," he added grimly, before the sheriff could think of an adequate comment, "I've a notion we both may have been outsmarted there. That may have been the general idea—that I pass on to you what was said, if I happened to meet you. And you didn't see anything of your *amigo* Elkins?"

The sheriff's face turned purple and he seemed to breathe with difficulty. Slade, apparently unmoved by these alarming symptoms, waited patiently for an answer.

"Yes, I saw him, and I wouldn't be surprised if you knew about that, too," Blevins said. "I saw him about three miles south of the pass as we came back to town; we caught up with him. He was driving a bunch of his blasted Boxed E cows he said somebody had wide-looped off his spread. Said they caught sight of the hellions not far from the Rio Grande and that when they saw they were tailed, they left the cows and headed across the river. He rounded up the beefs and shoved 'em back home."

Slade stared at the angry peace officer. There was little doubt in his mind now but that both he and Blevins had been nicely outsmarted. For Slade knew perfectly well that no cows had passed south along the Yucca Trail within twenty-four hours before he met Curly Bill Elkins and his bunch riding down from the north. All he said, however, was:

"The jigger I met told me he was chasing some rustled cattle."

"Of course," the sheriff replied sarcastically. "A perfect alibi for riding south hell-bent for election right after a robbery and murder. But I'll drop a loop on him yet, and on all you smooth hombres who think you can get by with anything. And when I do, it'll be just too bad! Now try and not shoot anybody else tonight; I'm going to bed, and I crave peace and quiet."

With an angry snort he stamped out. Slade struggled with a grin, although he was not in much of a mood for mirth. Walsh Price chuckled.

"But Lake's all right," he said. "He's an honest lawman and tries to do his duty as he sees it. And I reckon that's something."

"Yes, considerable," Slade replied. He rolled a cigarette, regarded the cowboy gravely.

"Price, while we're waiting for something more to eat, suppose you give me a notion what this is all about," he suggested. "I don't mind getting into the middle of a shindig when necessary, like I did tonight, but I feel I'm entitled to know what's the meaning of it."

"All right," said Price. "It ain't so much of a story, but it's got angles. To begin with, Manuel Peralta is a no-good wind spider."

"Rather a matter of personal opinion, usually," Slade interpolated. "Why?"

"Among other things, he fenced his holdings and ran sheep onto his hill pastures," Price said.

"Barbed wire has been coming to Texas for quite a few years now, and it's going to keep on coming, and you might as well admit it. There's nothing wrong with sheep if they're handled properly and not allowed to spoil range," Slade commented.

"Funny thing for a feller with the look of a cowhand to say," remarked the silent Tom Ord.

"Not necessarily, for one who isn't a hidebound cowhand with an ostrich habit of sticking his head in the ground and refusing to concede there' such things as progress and changing conditions because he can't see them," Slade retorted. "Texas *is* changing, and those who won't change with it are going to end up out the little end of the horn. All right, what else about Peralta?"

"Ord, you tell him," suggested Price. "You're the best talker when you get started, maybe because you usually keep a tight latigo on your jaw except when you've really got something to say."

"All right," Ord agreed, "I'll start at the beginning. The Snake S Ranch was first owned by a feller named Alvarez who got it by way of an old Spanish grant. Grant was sound, all right, and upheld by the Texas courts, like lots of them. He sold to *Don* Sebastian Gomez when Gomez was a young feller, a long time back. *Don* Sebastian was a real *don*, all right; pure Spanish blood, no Indian. He got married and had a couple of girls. Teresa was the oldest and Rosa was a couple of years younger. Rosa married another pure Spanish-blooded Mexican named Felipe Peralta, who owned a little spread to the north of *Don* Sebastian's holdings, the Boojer F. They had a kid and named him Manuel. Rosa died giving birth, and I guess Felipe Peralta did the best job he could of bringing up the kid without a mother, but it 'pears it wasn't good enough. Manuel was always a wild young hellion, and when Felipe Peralta got killed in a stampede, old *Don* Sebastian's troubles began, I reckon. He took on the chore of raising Manuel, of course. As I said, Manuel was a wild one. Gambled a lot, drank considerable, got into a few gun slingings, nothing overly serious. Finally, when he was twenty-one or two, about five years back, he busted up with *Don* Sebastian and went back to Boojer F, the spread his dad had left him, and set up in business for himself."

"How about *Don* Sebastian's other daughter?" Slade asked as Ord paused to drink some coffee.

"Coming to her," Ord replied. "Teresa married Bob Girton, *Don* Sebastian's range boss and sort of general manager. They had a kid, too, and named him Steve. Everybody connected with the Snake S seemed to get cashed in sudden and unexpected. Bob Girton tangled with a wide-looping bunch and leaned against the hot end of a passing slug. Reckon the shock of what happened killed Teresa. Anyhow, she didn't live long after that. So *Don* Sebastian had both grandsons on his hands. Steve never gave him any trouble, though; he was always a steady sort. Never mixed much but was always nice to every-body. A lot different from his cousin, Manuel Peralta, who always has a chip on his shoulder and hankers for somebody to knock it off."

"Is *Don* Sebastian Gomez still alive?" Slade asked.

"Nope," Ord replied soberly. "Been dead nearly two years now. As I said, everybody connected with the Snake S seems to cash in their chips the hard way. A couple of years back, *Don* Sebastian took a notion to go back to *mañana* land and visit his old home town where he was born, place called Jacinto, I believe, where he hadn't been for fifty years."

"Jacinto?" Slade repeated.

"Yep, that was it," said Ord. "Not so far south of the river, I gather. *Don* Sebastian took Steve Girton along, also a couple of hands and his old cook, who'd been with him a mighty long time. He set a heap of store by that cook, who used to be one of his riders. One day *Don* Sebastian's horse fell when he tied onto a mean steer, and the steer would have handed him his come-uppance if the cook hadn't bulldogged it and given *Don* Sebastian a chance to get up off the ground before he was skewered by the critter's horns. The cook—he wasn't a cook in those days—got a bad busted leg out of it and walked with a limp afterward and wasn't much good on a horse any more. So he went into the kitchen and helped look after things around the spread, too. Yep, him and *Don* Sebastian were mighty close *amigos*. But getting back to *Don* Sebastian: on the way to Jacinto his horse pitched him and cracked his skull. They buried him in Jacinto all in good order. Steve Girton brought back a death and burial certificate signed by the *alcalde*—the mayor —of Jacinto, and by the local medico. Everybody felt mighty bad about it, for *Don* Sebastian was as fine an old jigger as ever spit on the soil. When his will was read, it showed he'd left the Snake S to his grandson Steve Girton, which didn't surprise anybody much. He and Steve always got along, just like he and Manuel Peralta didn't, although he always seemed to have a soft spot in his heart for the young hellion—bailed him out of trouble a couple of times."

"How did Peralta take being cut off that way?" Slade asked.

"He didn't seem to mind overmuch, although he 'peared broke up over *Don* Sebastian getting cashed in that way," Ord replied. "Got on a blazing drunk right afterward and about wrecked the Last Chance Saloon down the street a ways. Funny, though, after that he sobered up a lot and hasn't hardly touched a drink since. Cut out most of his gambling, too, but he is as mean as ever, as you found out tonight."

"Do he and his cousin get along?" Slade asked.

Ord shook his head. "Never did," he replied. "I've a notion Steve tried to be nice to him but didn't get anywhere. They don't speak, and I've a notion Manuel is pretty sore at Steve for letting about all of *Don* Sebastian's old hands go; he hired some of them after Steve paid them off. Steve believes in efficiency, so he got rid of the deadwood and brought in young top hands from over east where he spent a lot of time during the past few years. He lives sort of high on the hog since *Don* Sebastian died. Makes trips over to the capital and to Dallas and other places. *Don* Sebastian must have had plenty of dinero stashed away in his strongbox. So you see, Slade, you tangled with a salty hombre tonight, and I'm scared you made a bad enemy; Manuel Peralta ain't the sort to take kind to a man-handling."

The other cowboys nodded in solemn agreement.

"Oh, I don't guess he'll be too much on the prod over a punch on the jaw; especially after he gets to thinking it over and realizes I stopped him from what would very likely have been a killing," Slade replied lightly.

"Don't be too sure," Walsh Price disagreed. "He ain't used to packing a licking, and I'm scairt it won't set over well with him. And he's got some salty jiggers working for him. That devil who buzzed the knife at you must be one of his hands. I didn't get a good enough look at the sidewinder to be sure, but I'd say it's mighty likely."

"Be that as it may, I've a notion that particular gent got a bellyful that'll hold him for a while," Slade returned. "A forty-five slug through the arm isn't easy to take."

Price nodded, but did not look convinced.

Chapter Four

"What about Curly Bill Elkins?" Slade suddenly asked. "Looks like I sort of got mixed up with him, too."

"Curly Bill ain't much help, but he's a puzzler," Price replied slowly. "Ain't much doubt but he used to operate down Mexico way and raised the devil plenty. But I gather he never came on this side of the river till a bit over a year ago when he showed up here and bought his Boxed E spread from the Ralston brothers who wanted to move to the Panhandle. So far, nobody's been able to pin anything off-color on him, though the robbery and wide-looping business has sure picked up hereabouts since he showed. Whenever anything happens, and plenty's happened in the past year, Sheriff Blevins is sure for certain that Curly is responsible, but he ain't ever been able to prove it."

"Sometimes a peace officer concentrates too much on some individual he mistakenly suspects, which makes it easy for the real culprit to get by with plenty," Slade observed thoughtfully.

"Guess that's right," conceded Price. "Elkins got himself a bad reputation down below the Line, so everybody looks at him sideways."

"What about the stage robbery of which the sheriff spoke?" Slade asked.

"That was a slick one," said Price. "They slipped on just one angle—the shotgun guard wasn't dead, although I reckon he looked it, with his head split open by a slug and his face all covered with blood. He was just a bit stunned, and watched the hellions bust open the stage and the strong-box. They were masked, but he said the feller who was giving the orders was a big jigger, tall and broad. He heard 'em say they were heading south for the Border."

Slade looked even more thoughtful. "The guard was only wounded, and they didn't make sure he was dead?" he asked.

"That's right, according to the way he told it," nodded Price. "He said they didn't pay any attention to him after he hit the ground. The big jigger walked over and took a look at him and after that paid him no mind."

"And he heard them say they were heading south on the Yucca Trail?"

Price nodded again.

"And just where was the robbery committed?" Slade asked.

"That's the funny part," Price replied. "It was almost in sight of Marlin, the railroad town up beyond the head of the valley, where the trail turns off and runs between canyon walls for a dozen miles. The hellions would have to go south from there. The guard cut one of the stage horses loose as soon as the devils were gone and hightailed to Marlin. They telegraphed Blevins and told him what had happened. Blevins played smart and set a guard of deputies down here to the south where the trail starts into the hills. The folks at Marlin guarded the upper end of the valley, and it looked like the hellions were trapped—there's no getting out of this crack to the east or west. But whoever pulled the chore didn't show up, and Blevins figured they must be holed up somewhere and was getting ready to comb the whole section when a prospector came by not long after daylight this morning and said he saw a bunch skalleyhooting down the Yucca south of the pass where the trail enters the hills. Blevins lit out south in a hurry, and you know the rest of what happened. How the hellions did it is a puzzler. They'd have had to pass over Manuel Peralta's holding and the Snake S, too, even to get to the pass where the deputies were stationed, much less get out that way. And no matter what Peralta was doing or wasn't doing, all the Snake S bunch were on the lookout for them. But they slid by somehow, or so it would appear."

"How did Elkins and his bunch trailing stolen cattle get out?" asked Slade.

Price shrugged his shoulders. "According to their yarn, they were down there in the hills trying to run down the thieves yesterday evening when the robbery was pulled off. No way to prove they were lying, if they were."

"Has Blevins any theory as to how the robbers might have eluded him?" Slade questioned.

Price looked uncomfortable. "Well, some folks think there might be a trail of some sort out of the valley by way of Peralta's Boojer F holding."

Slade nodded, but did not comment. He was not particularly impressed by Price's contention that there was no way out of the valley other than north and south by way of the Yucca Trail. When cowboys claimed familiarity with a section, usually their familiarity was restricted to the open range on which they did their work. Generally, the surrounding hill country was an unknown quantity, or at best, their knowledge went no further than certain defined trails. The outlaw fraternity, on the contrary, could be expected to be conversant with little known trails or openings in the broken country. Whoever was operating in the section was very likely thoroughly familiar with all its peculiarities. Slade had run up against such things before; doubtless the solution of the mystery which plagued the sheriff and his deputies was comparatively simple. Judgment on Manuel Peralta he held in abeyance. An unpopular individual was always suspect. Peralta might be in cahoots with Bill Elkins or somebody of like character, or then again he might not.

That Elkins was highly suspect, Slade was

willing to agree. Elkins had lied when he'd said he was trailing stolen cows south of where Slade had met him on the Yucca Trail. This caused El Halcon to regard him askance.

Incidentally, Slade's respect for Elkins' ingenuity had risen mightily. Caching a herd of cows somewhere to provide an alibi indicated unusual shrewdness and foresight. If Elkins was guilty of the murder and stage robbery, he had planned the outrage with care and well in advance of the actual perpetration—something a bit unusual in one of Elkins' type. Slade was familiar with his operations in Mexico, having been carefully briefed by Captain Jim McNelty, the Border Battalion commander, on Elkins' habits and mode of operation, before he set out for the Yucca Valley country to investigate that wily individual. Elkins' methods had always been of the direct type with scant subtlety.

Not that Slade underestimated Elkins; he had the reputation of being a cold killer, utterly ruthless and daring. Until Mexico got too hot to hold him, he cut a wide swath in the country south of the Rio Grande, but had never had anything definitely proven against him, although the Mexican authorities were convinced that he was guilty of law violations aplenty, so much so that the Governor of Chihuahua had finally issued orders that he be shot on sight. As a result, Elkins moved to Texas, where he assumed the guise of a respectable rancher. And so far nobody had been able to prove him otherwise, no matter what was suspected.

Walsh Price glanced at the clock over the bar and rose to his feet.

"Well, reckon it's about time to hit the hay," he announced. "I've had all the excitement I crave for one day."

"A good notion," Slade agreed. "I can stand a mite of ear pounding myself."

The other Tumbling R hands didn't object, and the party left the table. They were just passing the open back door, Price slightly in the lead, when Slade shot out a long arm and swept the cowboy clean off his feet. In the same movement he bounded convulsively to one side.

The room rocked to the crashing double roar of a shotgun. Fire streamed through the door opening. Buckshot screamed past so close, their breath fanned Slade's face. Tom Ord yelled with pain as a stray pellet nicked his ear.

Both Slade's guns let go with a crackling boom. The slugs screeched through the door, thudded into the jamb. Slade bounded forward, weaving and ducking. He reached the door and slewed sideways through it, hugging the building wall. He was in a dark and narrow alley that backed the Headlight.

Flame gushed from the darkness. A bullet smacked into the wall. Slade fired at the flash, raking the alley from side to side, leaped back and crouched low against the wall. Somewhere| in the darkness he could hear a queer tapping, as of boot heels beating a tattoo on the ground. The noise ceased, and all was quiet save for the pandemonium of yells and curses inside the saloon.

Slade slid a little to one side, peering and listening. He straightened cautiously, thumped his boot solidly against the ground and instantly changed position.

Nothing happened. He holstered one gun and stepped forward. In the murky edge of the bar of light streaming through the door, he could just make out a still form huddled on the ground. He took another cautious step forward; there was neither sound nor movement from the body.

Men began pouring out the door. Walsh Price came shouldering through the crowd, gun in hand.

"Bring a light," Slade told him.

One was forthcoming in a moment, a bracket lamp from the wall. Its flame revealed a man's body lying on his back in the dust. His glazing eyes stared upward from his swarthy face. Around his left arm a handkerchief was bound.

"It's that sidewinder who flung the knife!" whooped Price. "He won't fling another! You drilled him dead center this time, Slade. Look, there's his shotgun over there, and here's his six. Didn't I tell you to watch out for Peralta?"

"Nothing to tie up Peralta or anybody else with this, so far as I can see," Slade demurred. "Remember, I gunned this jigger. He may have figured he had a pretty strong personal reason for wanting to even up the score."

"Maybe," grunted Price, "but I still got my notions."

"Bring him inside, and let's see if anybody can identify him or who he was associated with," Slade said.

The dead man was carried into the saloon and laid on the floor. Contrary to his expectations, Price was forced to admit that he did not recognize him as one of Manuel Peralta's employees. He couldn't recall ever seeing him before. Nor could anybody else remember seeing him with the Peralta outfit, or any place else, for that matter.

Slade untied the handkerchief bound around the dead man's arm and examined the wounded member.

"Just a nick," he said to Price. "Sliced through the flesh and didn't touch the bone. Reckon he hardly felt it after he got over the shock."

He gazed at the insignificant wound. Passing strange, he thought, that the man should go in for cold-blooded murder and take such a desperate chance to avenge so trifling a hurt. However, he did not make mention of the matter.

"Ain't got much of a Mexican look to him," said Ord, peering closely at the dark face. "Heap of Indian blood, though, I'd say."

"Got an Apache look to him," remarked Price. "See those cheek bones and that nose. Face mighty broad, too."

"Not many Apaches left in Texas," somebody observed. "Most of 'em over New Mexico and Arizona way. What'll we do with the hellion?"

"Lug him into the back room behind the bar and cover him with a blanket," said the fat and mustached owner of the Headlight. "Reckon the sheriff and Doc Potter will want to hold an inquest over the horned toad. A plumb waste of time, if you ask me."

Slade took the dead man's shoulders, Price his feet. With the proprietor waddling after them, they carried him into the back room and deposited him in a corner.

"Shut the door and keep the crowd out," Slade told the saloonkeeper. "I'd like to give him a closer once-over."

The man's clothing was regulation range garb, with nothing to distinguish it. His gun and the shotgun, which Tom Ord brought along, were ordinary, of standard make and usual calibre. Nor did his pockets reveal anything of interest. Slade was about to give up the search when his hand felt something bulky under the fellow's shirt. He investigated and drew forth a plump money belt which disgorged a shower of shiny twenty-dollar gold pieces.

"Whe-e-ew!" whistled Price. "Look at all that dinero! The hellion sure must have made a killing recent; he never glommed onto all those yellow boys at forty per, that's sure for certain."

Slade counted the money and handed it to the saloonkeeper. "Put it in the safe and hold it for the sheriff," he said. "And by the way, if I was you fellows, I wouldn't talk about this. The sheriff might want to keep it under cover till he gets a line on where it came from."

The advice was received with solemn nods. The Headlight owner was stowing the gold in his safe, which stood in a corner of the room, when a voice bawled outside the closed door:

"Here comes the sheriff, late as usual!"

"Oh, Lord!" Price groaned hollowly. "*Now* are we going to catch it!"

The door banged open and Sheriff Blevins stalked in, looking in an even worse temper than earlier in the evening. He glared at Slade.

"So!" he barked. "Still at it, eh? Now what you got to say for yourself?"

Slade didn't get a chance to say anything at the moment. Price, Ord, Perkins and the saloonkeeper all began talking at once, while the sheriff, unable to get a word in edgewise, waved his arms as if conducting the music.

"And that's how it stands!" Walsh Price stormed in conclusion. "A respectable citizen can't ride into this blasted town without some horned toad trying to knife and gun him! Why didn't you go looking for this sidewinder after he flung the knife, instead of letting him run around loose and come nigh to doing for all of us with his infernal scattergun?"

"Respectable citizen!" howled the sheriff. "He's a blasted owlhoot if there ever was one!"

"Can you prove it? Can you prove it?" yelled Price.

"Of course I can't prove it or I'd lock him up right now," retorted the sheriff. "But everybody knows he is."

"Everybody!" bawled Price. "Who the blankety-blank-blank is everybody? A bunch of supposed-to-be-lawmen as shy of brains as a terrapin is of feathers! Got killings to his credit, you say? To his *credit* is right! Here's a sample right here. Shouldn't take the law in his own hands, eh? Suppose he should have filed a complaint with you while that hellion kept on pulling trigger out in the dark! When there ain't no law, it's up to the right sort of folks to *make* law!"

The sheriff swore appallingly, and Price was about to start all over again when Slade's musical voice interrupted.

"Seems to me we're getting exactly nowhere with all this palaver," he said. "Sheriff, the saloonkeeper has something to show you—he was just stashing it away when you came in—that I think you may find interesting. I believe you said the stage that was robbed yesterday was packing payroll money?"

"That's right, for the mines," replied the sheriff.

"Hard money?"

"Uh-huh." The sheriff nodded. "Most of the mine workers are Mexicans, and they don't take to paper over well; prefer hard money, gold and silver."

Slade gestured to the saloonkeeper, who produced the double eagles taken from the slain drygulcher and passed them to the sheriff.

"New stuff," Blevins muttered. "The money in the strongbox had just come from the Marlin bank and the chances are it was new. Can't identify coin, of course, but I wouldn't be surprised if this was part of the loot."

"How about the minting date?" Slade suggested. "If they happen all to be the same it might mean something."

Sheriff Blevins examined the coins and shook his head. "Different dates," he said.

"So that's out," Slade observed, "but it does seem sort of funny that the hellion should be packing better than five hundred dollars in new money."

"You're right about that," growled the sheriff. "It's sure for certain he never got it honest."

"And if by any chance it is part of the proceeds

of the robbery, it would mean the robbers headed into town," Slade persisted.

Sheriff Blevins shot him a quick look. "Would seem that way," he admitted reluctantly.

"While you were chasing your tail through the hills," Walsh Price observed sarcastically.

The sheriff looked angry, then cooled off. "If this happens to be part of the loot, I guess that's about the size of it," he said quietly.

"And if it is, it means you're up against a mighty smooth outfit," Slade interpolated.

"No doubt about that," the sheriff conceded wearily. "Well, I reckon there's nothing more to be done tonight. Cover the body up, Kettlebelly," he told the saloonkeeper. "Doc Potter, the coroner, will want to hold an inquest tomorrow. You fellers be at my office at ten; that's early enough. And now will you young squirts *please* go to bed? I crave sleep."

"We were headed that way when that devil threw those blue whistlers at us," said Price. "See you tomorrow, Lake."

As they made their way to the rooming house, Price chuckled.

"Slade, you sure quieted the old man down," he observed. "Don't know how you did it; he was rarin' and chargin' till you started talking to him."

"He's all right," Slade smiled. "And he's got his troubles. Small wonder he paws sod now and then. Well, here we are; see you in the morning."

Chapter Five

The following morning, after due deliberation, the coroner's jury held Slade justified in killing the unrecognized drygulcher and allowed he'd done a good chore. "Almost as good as the ones the sheriff ain't been doing of late," the foreman appended sarcastically.

Which remark did not improve that harassed peace officer's temper.

Steve Girton, *Don* Sebastian Gomez' grandson and owner of the Snake S Ranch, was present at the inquest. He made a point of personally congratulating Slade.

"But I'm afraid you made a bad enemy last night," he added.

"You mean your cousin Manuel Peralta?" Slade asked.

Girton shrugged his broad shoulders. "I mean whoever set that killer on you," he replied evasively. "Whoever did it is not likely to be discouraged by a failure."

"You're probably right," Slade agreed soberly, but did not comment further.

Girton nodded and walked over to talk with Sheriff Blevins. Walsh Price joined Slade and suggested the Headlight and a drink. Slade was agreeable, and they repaired to the saloon. Standing at the far end of the bar was Curly Bill Elkins and three companions Slade recognized as members of the bunch he had met on the Yucca Trail the day before.

Elkins twinkled his black eyes at Slade, waved his hand and grinned. Not to be outdone in courtesy, Slade waved back. The Tumbling R cowboys glowered and ignored Elkins' greeting.

"The nerve of that sidewinder!" fumed Price. "He knows what everybody's thinking and just don't give a hang. Rides into town as if he owned the pueblo."

"Reckon folks are not doing their thinking out loud when Bill is around," remarked Tom Ord. "He's a cold proposition."

"He'll end up the prime attraction at a necktie party," Price predicted wrathfully. "See if he don't."

"Maybe," said Ord, "but I've a notion Bill Elkins will never stretch rope. If it comes to a showdown, he'll go out with both guns blazing, or I'm a lot mistaken."

Slade was inclined to think Ord was right.

As he sipped his drink, Slade studied Elkins' face in the back bar mirror. It was a powerful face but, Slade felt, not particularly intelligent. In build and general appearance Elkins reminded him of another gentleman who had enjoyed the soubriquet, Curly Bill—Curly Bill Brocius of Tombstone, Arizona, fame.

But Curly Bill Brocius had had John Ringo to plan and direct his depredations. Without Ringo to do his thinking for him, the notorious Arizona outlaw leader would have been only a minor nuisance. Slade wondered if the parallel might not hold good here. Elkins too might be the field man for someone with a lot more brains who stayed discreetly in the background and pulled the wires. Well, it was up to him to find out; that was what he was here for.

Walsh Price plucked at Slade's sleeve and drew him aside. "Feller," he said, "we've got to be getting back to the spread before the old man has a duck fit. But I want a word with you first. I've took considerable of a shine to you, and so have the other boys. I'm range boss of the Tumbling R, and the old man lets me handle all the hiring. With the roundup season right on top of us and shipping herds to line up, there are busy times ahead and we can use a few more top-hands. So if you'd like to sign up for a job riding for as fine a cattleman as ever was, I'm all set to say it's okay; that is, if you aren't just passing through and figure to coil your twine in this section for a spell."

Slade considered a moment. The offer was not without attractions. It would give him an excuse to stick around and also an opportunity to study the valley and its conditions. There was little doubt in his mind but that a well organized criminal outfit was working the section; if not curbed it would very likely spread out and achieve formidable proportions. It was his chore to put a stop to any such development. So he nodded, and said:

"Thanks for the offer, Price, and the chances are I'll take you up on it. I'd like to loaf around a day or so longer and rest up after a hard ride, but I'll be seeing you soon, I expect."

"Fine; we'll let it go at that," said Price. "Ride up to the spread when you're a mind to. No trouble to get there—just follow the Yucca Trail. For about ten miles it runs across Steve Girton's Snake S. Then you come to Manuel Peralta's wire that fences in his holding, the Boojer F, to the left. Our south pasture begins there on the right. Four miles more and you turn off to our ranchhouse, which sets in a grove of pinions three miles to the east of the main trail. Can't miss it."

"The Yucca Trail runs on to Marlin, the railroad town, doesn't it?" Slade asked.

"That's right," said Price. "Half a dozen miles past where the fork turns to our *casa* it cuts into the hills and follows them on to Marlin, thirty miles to the northwest."

"Trail doesn't run all the way through the valley, then," Slade commented.

"At the north end she's boxed," Price explained. "No getting up the cliffs there, and no getting up the side walls, either, past where the Yucca turns into the hills. The Yucca's an old trail; the Lord only knows who rode it first. Might have started out as an old buffalo track years and years back when the critters were traveling north and south from one feeding ground to another. Or maybe the Indians beat it out first. Anyhow, it's been here a long time. Well, I'll have to be moving. Hope we'll see you soon."

Slade went back to the bar and continued to study Elkins and his companions, who seemed well on the way to getting roaring drunk. Elkins' face was flushed and there was a mad gleam in his eyes. Slade decided that he had an uncontrollable temper and was as explosive as dynamite, characteristics that were doubtless accentuated by alcohol. The three men with him were hard-looking propositions, and it was obvious that they did not wear their hardware for ornamental purposes.

The saloon was filling up, and Slade frequently made room for new arrivals, most of them jovial young cowhands who showed their appreciation of his courtesy by invitations to have one. Slade declined the invitations with thanks, tipping his nearly full glass. For he amusedly realized that if he accepted he would soon be in a condition similar to that which Curly Bill Elkins and his companions were fast approaching.

As a result of his steadily shifting position, he worked down the bar until he was next to Elkins and his group. They were busy talking among themselves, however, and accorded him no attention.

Suddenly Slade realized that the jabber of talk along the bar was stilling to a curious silence. He glanced around and saw Sheriff Lake Blevins striding down the bar in his direction. The sheriff did not speak to him, however; his eyes were fixed on Elkins, and his mouth was a hard line under his mustache. He paused within arm's length of the Boxed E owner, who regarded him hostilely. Slade toyed with his filled whiskey glass and awaited developments.

"Elkins," the sheriff said harshly, "I think the best thing you can do is get out of town."

"Why?" Elkins asked, his voice deceptively mild. His three companions fanned out a little from him.

"Because you're not wanted here, that's why," the sheriff retorted. "We can do without your kind, and besides, you're getting drunk and all set to make trouble. Get going!"

"Listen, lawman," Elkins growled, "if you've got a warrant for me, serve it. If you ain't, 'tend to your own blankety-blank business and don't go sticking your long nose into other people's."

Sheriff Blevins flushed scarlet and his eyes blazed. Whether he really intended to draw on Elkins, Slade was never quite sure, but he did drop his hand to his gun butt.

Elkins gave a yell of rage. His hand flashed down and up, and he was fast, almighty fast. Slade heard the hammer of the big single-action click back to full cock.

Chapter Six

But before Elkins could quite clear leather, he got the contents of Slade's whiskey glass in his eyes. Utterly blinded, he howled with pain, let go of his gun and pawed at his face with both hands. His companions, fanned out on either side, instantly pulled, and the ball was open. Men fled wildly in every direction as red spurts flickered through the wisps of smoke. The air quivered to the roar of the reports, the yells and curses and the crash of smashed furniture.

Seconds later, Walt Slade, thumbs hooked over the hammers of his Colts, blood trickling down the side of his face, one shirt sleeve a flapping ruin, peered through the smoke fog with icy eyes.

Two of Elkins' men were down, one with a bullet-smashed shoulder, the other with a punctured thigh. The third, his hands high in the air, one streaming crimson, was yelling, "Don't shoot! Don't shoot!"

Curly Bill, still blinded, was staggering about moaning and swearing. Sheriff Blevins belatedly had his gun out and looked as if he wanted to use it on somebody.

Slade holstered one gun, seized Elkins by the

shirt front, shook him till his teeth rattled and slammed him against the bar.

"Be still and don't try to start anything, or I'll break your infernal neck!" he told him. "Get some water and wash his eyes out," he ordered a bartender who bobbed up from where he had crouched behind the "mahogany."

The drink juggler hurried to obey, and after a few moments' ministrations with a bar towel and water, Elkins was able to see from his swollen and reddened eyes. He glared at Slade and swore feebly.

"What were you trying to do, get yourself hanged for murder?" said the Ranger. "That's just what you'd be facing now if I hadn't stopped you."

"Blast you, I guess you're right," Elkins mumbled as he rubbed his smarting eyes. "But why did that old hellion have to jump me that way? I wasn't bothering anybody."

"He's got something there, Blevins," Slade told the sheriff. "You went off half-cocked."

"I guess you're right again," growled the sheriff, "but that hellion makes me see red every time I clap eyes on him." He glared at Elkins, who returned the glare, albeit with a watery one.

"Won't somebody get a doctor?" wailed the man with the shoulder wound. "I'm bleeding to death!"

"Guess not," Slade said as he knelt beside him. "Bring some more bar towels and I'll patch them up till the doctor gets here," he directed. "Neither one hurt bad. Blevins, send somebody for Doc Potter. And put your gun away; you won't be needing it."

Everybody, including the sheriff, hastened to obey this tall cowhand who had usurped all the authority in sight. Slade went to work on the injured men and had the bleeding under control before the doctor arrived. He swabbed the nick in his own scalp with a handkerchief and shook his head ruefully over his ruined shirt.

"Lucky I've got a spare in my saddle pouch," he observed. "This kind of shindig is always expensive." He bent a cold gaze on Elkins' bandaged and crestfallen henchmen.

"Don't try it again," he warned them. "Next time it won't be just hands, legs and shoulders." Turning his back on the discomfited Boxed E bunch, he walked to the far end of the bar and ordered a drink.

After Doc Potter finished with them, the casualties hobbled out the back door. Sheriff Blevins joined Slade at the bar.

"Guess you saved my bacon, all right," he said. "Elkins would have killed me."

"Maybe," Slade conceded.

"No maybe about it," declared the sheriff. "When that hellion's drunk, he's a madman.

"Did you mean what you said about legs and shoulders?" he added curiously.

"I did," Slade replied. "I considered the whole affair a bit of darn foolishness and didn't see any sense in killing somebody if I didn't have to."

"You'd have done the community a big favor if you'd drilled all four of them dead center," growled the sheriff.

"Possibly," Slade answered, "but you could be wrong. Elkins may be all you claim, but it's not the Texas way and not the American way to judge a man guilty before he's proven so. Elkins has a right to his day in court the same as any other man."

"I guess that's so," the sheriff admitted grudgingly.

"But you took one heck of a chance, picking the spots where you'd hit those hellions instead of just mowing them down," he said.

"Not so much," Slade disagreed. "Contrary to popular opinion, that kind is usually nothing extra with a gun. Elkins is different," he added thoughtfully. "He pulled mighty fast, so fast that I figured the only way to stop him in time was with that whiskey; a glass of alcohol in the eyes will throw a man off balance as effectively as a slug, and sometimes it's quicker."

"You think as fast as you pull, and that's saying plenty," observed Blevins. "Anyhow, I'm mighty beholden to you, and if you're ever in trouble and need a helpin' hand, call on me and I'll do all I can."

"Thank you, I appreciate that and won't forget it," Slade replied gravely.

Sheriff Blevins offered a little well meant advice. "Why don't you stop mavericking around over the country, always taking the chance of getting into serious trouble, and settle down?" he said. "Right here is a good section for an up-and-coming young feller. No better cattle country in Texas, and you wouldn't have any trouble tying onto a good job of riding. The Tumbling R boys 'pear to have took to you, and Price wouldn't have any trouble persuading Rance Rutledge to sign you on. He'd be a good man to work for, Rutledge; none better. And if you must go looking for excitement, later on I'll appoint you a deputy and you'll find plenty."

"Thank you again," Slade answered, his gay, reckless eyes abruptly very serious. "I'll think it over."

"Do that," said the sheriff. "Well, I've got to be getting back to the office—work to do." With a nod he departed. Slade turned back to the bar, his untasted drink in his hand, and conned over the recent hectic happenings. He had not altered his opinion of Curly Bill Elkins, a not too bright, quick-tempered brawler. Dangerous, all right, but certainly not the man to plan and execute a complicated maneuver. If, as the sheriff undoubtedly was convinced, Elkins was operating in the section, he was not doing it on his own. More than ever Slade believed there was a smarter man behind Elkins doing his thinking for him. But who?

Slade's thoughts turned to Manuel Peralta. Slade felt he had brains. And he also was on the sheriff's suspect list, according to what Walsh Price and the other Tumbling R cowboys had said. There was a possibility that Peralta, smarting under injustices, might have worked out a subtle scheme of revenge on his neighbors, at the same time lining his own pockets. Such things had happened before. Elkins might well be Peralta's field man.

All of which, of course, was mere conjecture. So far as he had been able to learn, there was nothing definite against either Peralta or Elkins. All that could be said against Peralta, so far as Slade knew, was that he was a rather wild young man who had antagonized the majority of the ranch owners of the section by fencing his holdings and bringing in sheep. And Slade did not forget that he had heard but one side of the Peralta story. Walsh Price and his companions could hardly be considered unprejudiced narrators.

Much the same reasoning applied to Curly Bill Elkins. There was no doubt but that the

Boxed E owner had done plenty of swaller-forking south of the Rio Grande; but he might have reformed after he came north and decided that henceforth he would be an honest rancher.

Slade placed his glass on the bar and left to have a little talk with Shadow.

All eyes followed the tall form through the swinging doors, and as soon as he had disappeared, heated discussions broke out.

"In my opinion—take it for what it's worth—this section is going to have a new owlhoot boss," said Kettlebelly Watson, the Headlight owner. "And if that big jigger takes over, gentlemen, trouble will be a-poppin' for fair. Did you ever see such gun-slingin'? Those irons just growed in his hands, and I don't think he missed a single shot. When he blasted the gun out of that tall hellion's hand, he shot over Curly Bill's shoulder to do it and didn't plug Bill. That was shooting!"

"I've heard a good deal about him," remarked an old cowhand. "They say he always manages to get in with sheriffs, just like he did with Blevins today. Blevins would have gotten it if it hadn't been for him. Guess he won't forget it, either."

"Blevins won't let that stand in his way if he catches him at something off-color," somebody protested. "Lake Blevins is an honest man."

"Sure he's an honest man," answered the

cowhand. "But how are you going to feel about a feller who keeps you from getting killed and risks his own life to do it? Sure Lake is honest, but he's human, too."

Others nodded agreement. "I'll have to say if I was in Blevins' boots, I'd sort of look the other way a mite, maybe," said Kettlebelly.

"I've heard it said that he ain't no owlhoot at all," somebody else observed.

"Then what is he?"

"Don't ask me. Maybe he is an owlhoot, but just the same I'd say he's a man to ride the river with."

There was no disagreement.

Chapter Seven

Before repairing to the stable where Shadow was domiciled, Slade decided to look the town over a bit.

Sotol Avenue, as it was called, was Chino's main street and a busy one. General stores and other shops were sandwiched between saloons and gambling houses. The business section of the street was covered by wooden arcades supported by posts at the edge of the board sidewalk, which provided a grateful shade from the sun. Under these awnings a jostling crowd moved to and fro. There were cowboys in rangeland garb, shop-keepers and their employees in "store clothes," Mexican *vaqueros* in black velvet pantaloons, tight-fitting short jackets and sombreros encrusted with much silver. Peons with *serapes* across their shoulders and grass sandals on their feet shuffled along. Slade saw a Chinese or two and several dark-faced Indians of Comanche or Yaqui blood.

Chino was undoubtedly a prosperous pueblo. In addition to the trade for the town provided by the ranches of the valley there were producing mines in the hills which brought their ore to the Chino stamp mills to be crushed and bought their supplies in Chino. Slade knew that there were also many old abandoned mines in the hills that dated back to the days when imperial Spain ruled the Big Bend country as part of a vast New World empire. Now the ancient galleries that had once resounded to the thudding of picks and the scraping of shovels were given over to the coyote, the owl and the bat. The miles of tunnels stretched this way and that through the hills, as the miners followed the veins of ore.

Slade walked slowly, pausing to glance in store windows, noting the faces of passersby. He had covered most of the main business district when he saw two men standing on a corner conversing earnestly. One was Curly Bill Elkins, the other Manuel Peralta. As Slade drew near, slowing his pace, Peralta made an angry gesture, turned and walked rapidly away. Elkins gazed after him a moment, shrugged his shoulders and entered a nearby saloon.

Slade strolled on, his eyes thoughtful. What had they been talking about? he wondered. It looked as if there had been an argument and Peralta had stalked off in a huff. A more absorbing question— what did the pair have in common?

The wooden awnings ended and the sun poured down hotly. Slade walked a little farther, glanced at the sky. It was mid-afternoon. He turned and retraced his steps to the stable which housed Shadow.

"What do you say we take a little amble?" he

asked the big black. "I think it wouldn't be a bad notion to give this gulch a bit of a once-over; we don't know much about it yet."

Shadow was agreeable, and Slade got the rig on him and left the stable. He paused at a store long enough to replenish his supply of staple provisions and rode north on the Yucca Trail.

Yucca Valley was fine rangeland. It was heavily grassed, with plenty of groves and thickets. The ground was rolling, and little streams flashed in the sun.

For quite a while Slade saw only cattle bearing the Snake S burn, and plenty of them, all in good condition. He had gathered that the Snake S spread occupied the whole south end of the valley, extending up it for better than ten miles and being the biggest holding in the section, with old Rance Rutledge's Tumbling R a close second. A valuable property, all right; Steve Girton's inheritance had certainly been worthwhile, and Manuel Peralta could hardly be blamed if he resented being cut off by his grandfather's will.

As he rode, Slade better appreciated Walsh Price's contention that there was no way out of the valley except by the Yucca Trail. To all appearances it was completely walled in by towering cliffs or precipitous mountain slopes, with the broad Yucca flowing up the middle and dwindling to a gray thread in the distance.

Autumn was at hand, and the scene was one of

exquisite beauty. The hills were warrior monks clad in scarlet and gold, marching along the sky-line. The grass heads were tipped with amethyst and the hollows were bronzed with fading ferns. Overhead the sky was a deep blue, with the great sun a disc of flame, while the streams edged the green garment of the rangeland with silver. Birds sang in the thickets and little animals went about their affairs in peace and harmony.

"A pretty country, Shadow," Slade remarked to his horse. "You'd think that folks would absorb some of this beauty and be kind to one another, glad to share the plenty this great land of ours affords for all. Race and creed and the color of a man's skin shouldn't count for much, and folks ought to be willing to share and help one another. It isn't always so, but it's getting better as the years go by. Now and then there's a setback, like here in this valley, but it doesn't last. Just like the tide, it rolls forward and then recedes, but each time it rolls a little farther, and each time when it recedes it leaves a wider stretch of clean, washed beach. You can't rush things, feller, but just give them time, just give them time!"

Slade had covered quite a few miles when he saw Manuel Peralta's wire stretching westward, turning at right angles and then running parallel to the trail. He noted that while the eastern portion of the Boojer F was excellent rangeland, to the west were hills and their rocky slopes, grass-grown but too steep for cattle, and dotted with sheep. He saw, too, that inner lines of wire fenced off pastures. Evidently Peralta knew his business and transferred his woolies from one feeding ground to another before they could damage the grass by eating it down to the roots and cutting the roots with their chisel-like feet. Handled so, sheep did not damage range and throve on ground which was no good for cows. Slade knew that many cattlemen, recognizing the fact and seeing the profit in sheep, had utilized their formerly worthless hill pastures in such fashion. It was new to the Big Bend country, and bound to kick up a row until the stubborn old-timers saw the error of their ways and fell in line with the progress they couldn't hope to retard. Manuel Peralta was a pioneer in Yucca valley and, like all pioneers, found himself beset by difficulties.

As to what else he might be, Slade didn't know. He seemed to be at least on speaking terms with Curly Bill Elkins, and Slade was decidedly dubious about Elkins. But there might well be a perfectly legitimate reason for him talking to the Boxed E owner, and the manner in which he had abruptly terminated the conversation hinted at a certain amount of disagreement between the pair, no matter what the explanation of their associa-tion. Slade still felt that his judgment of Peralta must be held in abeyance.

Slade had passed about a mile of Peralta's fence when he sighted a belt of grove that continued for some distance and obscured the trail ahead. He was perhaps two hundred yards from the beginning of the growth when his keen ears caught the sound of drumming hoofs. Another moment and a band of fast-riding horsemen, nearly a score in number, burst from the grove and swept toward him. The sunlight gleamed on gun handles and the butt plates of rifles protruding from their saddle boots. He slowed Shadow's gait and watched the approach of the compact body of riders, whose dark faces were set in grim lines and whose eyes gleamed with purpose.

Suddenly a wild yell sounded.

"It is he! It is he! Forward, *amigos*!"

Whooping and bellowing, the horsemen spurred their mounts to greater effort. Slade reined in, fished the makings from his shirt pocket and began manufacturing a cigarette. Shadow laid back his ears and bared his teeth.

"Take it easy," Slade told him. "No sense in starting a shindig with a couple of dozen. Take it easy!"

The horsemen charged ahead, jerked their mounts to a slithering halt. Sinewy hands reached for Slade, seized his arms, his shoulders, patted his back. He was completely hemmed in by grinning faces.

"*Capitan*!" exclaimed a tall young fellow, who

spoke the precise English of the Mission-taught Mexican. "*Capitan*, I am Estaban Cartinas, range boss for *Don* Manuel Peralta. And look, *Capitan*! Here is Pedro Garcia whom you saved from death at the hands of those evil ones."

"Guess it wouldn't have been that bad," Slade replied, recognizing the Mexican cowhand he had rescued from the Tumbling R cowboys. "I expect they would only have roughed him up a bit. Had no business doing that, though."

Estaban Cartinas' face darkened and he shook his fist in the air.

"But the day of reckoning is at hand," he said. "Those *ladrones* have sent word that they await us in Chino and have dared us to ride to town and meet them. We accept the challenge; we will fight!"

"Oh, no, you won't!" Slade answered. "You're not going to start any range war in this section if I can prevent it, and I think I can. Who told you the Tumbling R bunch is waiting for you in town?"

"One rode to our *casa* this morning with the word," Estaban replied.

"Who was he?" Slade asked.

"*Capitan*, I do not know; I had never before seen him," Estaban said. "He brought us the friendly warning and then rode on."

"He did, eh?" Slade retorted. "A *very* friendly warning, it would seem. Now what the devil is this all about?"

"*Capitan*, I do not know," said Estaban, "but they have threatened us, and we will not be cowed. We have been patient, patient for long, and have ignored the insults and the slights. But the attack on Pedro and now this is too much. We fight."

The others shouted approval of this bold speech, but Slade quickly stilled the tumult.

"Quiet, hombres," he said. "There is something very strange about all this. I just rode from town, and the Tumbling R hands are not there. In fact, the three who were there rode back this way hours ago. Quiet, and give me a chance to think."

A *vaquero* uttered an exclamation. "Hark!" he ejaculated. "Somebody comes!"

Slade heard it, too, a drumming of hoofs from the north. Several persons were coming, and coming fast. Slade had a very good notion who they were.

"Stay where you are," he snapped at the *vaqueros*, and sent Shadow moving forward a score of paces; he reined around in the middle of the trail, from where he could watch in both directions.

The hoofbeats grew louder. Out of the grove bulged Walsh Price with a dozen or more cowhands at his back.

"There they are!" bawled Tom Ord as the horses foamed to a halt. "Get set, boys!" Cowboys and *vaqueros* clutched their weapons.

"Hold it!" Slade thundered. "Price, Estaban, I'll kill the first man who makes a move! Hold it, I say!"

A chorus of oaths and exclamations in two languages sprinkled the air. Slade's great voice drowned out all the other sounds.

"What's the matter with you, Price?" he demanded. "Have you gone completely loco? What are you on the prod about?"

"Those hellions sent us word if we came to town they aimed to blow us from under our hats!" howled Price. "We ain't backing down for nobody! We'll ride to town when we're a mind to! Might as well settle this thing right now!"

"Shut up!" Slade told him. "Try it and I'll guarantee *you* won't ever know how it was settled. Who brought you word that the Boojer F *vaqueros* were waiting for you in town?"

"A feller rode up to the ranchhouse a little while back and said he thought we ought to know what was in the wind, on the chance two or three of us riding to town might get mowed down."

"Who was he? Where is he now?" Slade asked.

"Why, we didn't know him," Price confessed. "He said he signed on with the Bar A, up at the head of the valley, last week. He rode on to his spread after he told us."

"He did, eh?" Slade said with withering scorn. "And you fell for it, just as these addle-pates over here fell for the same phony yarn from the same horned toad! Come ahead, slow. Get down here with the others, where I can keep an eye on all of you. Come ahead, I said!"

The Tumbling R hands hesitated, glaring at the *vaqueros*, who returned the glares with interest.

"Come on; what are you afraid of?" Slade said.

"We ain't afraid of nothin', much less those jiggers!" Price shouted in reply. From the ranks of the *vaqueros* arose a chorus of jeers.

The situation was tense, packed with dynamite. Slade regretfully opened his lips to roll forth the words that would give pause to any gathering between the Red Silver and the Rio Grande—

In the name of the State of Texas! Under the authority of the Texas Rangers!

But he didn't need to voice them. The stern personality of the man confronting them was enough for the reluctant Tumbling R hands, who evidently felt it best to obey. Slade sat perfectly quiet in his saddle, but the thumbs of his slender hands were hooked over his double cartridge belts and close to the black butts of his guns. Perhaps Walsh Price and Tom Ord, who were in the front ranks and had seen Slade in action, felt a mite uncomfortable. At any rate, they sent their horses forward, the others jostling along behind them. Slade spoke to Shadow, and the big black moved backward, keeping time with the advancing punchers. Slade pulled over to one side and waited until the two factions were practically grouped together.

"All right," he said, "that's enough." The moving horses jingled to a stop. Cowboys and *vaqueros* slanted glances at one another, but nobody made a hostile move. Slade regarded them in silence for a long moment. Then he lit into them for fair.

"Of all the loco, sway-backed jugheads, you're the limit. I've seen some prize specimens in my time, but you take the cake. You should be playing with strings of spools or cutting out paper dolls instead of riding range. I don't think either outfit could tell skunks from housecats, and you need a wet nurse. If the collective brains of the lot of you were dynamite, there wouldn't be enough to blow my hat off my head. Estaban, I believe your boss is in town, isn't he?"

"That is right, *Capitan*," replied the Boojer F range boss.

"And, Price, where is your boss?"

"He rode over to the Bradded Dash to spend the night with old Cale Dalton," Price mumbled.

"And the pair of you aimed to start a row that would embroil the whole section without consulting the men for whom you work! I think you'll both hear from them later."

Price and Estaban looked decidedly uncomfortable. Apparently they didn't anticipate with relish the coming interviews with their irate employers.

"Isn't there anybody among you with the intelligence to realize it was a plant," Slade resumed, "to see that somebody is deliberately trying to start trouble between you? Who and why I don't know, yet, but I intend to find out. All right; get going back the way you came, the lot of you, and try and act like human beings instead of a bunch of feather-headed hydrophobia skunks. Get going, I say! We've had enough of this kind of foolishness for one day."

Without argument, the two outfits obeyed, jostling along in a tight group. Slade followed, a dozen paces to the rear.

Chapter Eight

Presently they came to a gate in the fence, which was swung open to let the *vaqueros* stream through. And it was, "So long, Estaban!" "So long, Pedro!" Take care of yourself, Juan!" "Be seeing you, Felipe!" on the one side, and "*Adios*, Walsh!" "*Adios*, Perkins!" "*Gracias*, James!" "*Hasta luego*, Tomas!" on the other.

"*Capitan*," Estaban called to Slade, "will you come to the *casa* and dine?"

"Not today," the Ranger declined. "I've got to see that these other jiggers get home safely, too. They're like you, not to be trusted out alone this late. But I'll be seeing you soon."

Laughter greeted the sally, and the Tumbling R hands rode on.

"Slade," Walsh Price said in a complaining voice, "how the devil do you do the things you do? You grab thirty hellions on the prod and all set to go and send them packin' off together like so many wooly lambs! How do you do it?"

"Perhaps," Slade smiled, "I just give them an opportunity to see that there's really not very much difference between them, and plenty of good in all of them if it's just given a chance to sprout."

Price shook his head. "I still can't understand

it," he declared, "but what the devil's the meaning of what happened, anyhow?"

"It's an old owlhoot trick," Slade replied thoughtfully. "Set two factions on the prod against one another and let them blame each other for everything off-color that happens. While they're so busy gunning for each other, the hellions slide in and skim off the cream. Yes, an old trick, but it works."

"I'd like to get my hands on the devil who brought us the word Estaban and his bunch were all set to make trouble," growled Price. "I'd make trouble for *him!*"

"I doubt if you'll get the chance," Slade replied. "Very likely, after finishing his chore, he kept right on riding. Of course he might circle back to where he came from."

"And I wonder where the devil that is," grunted Price.

"Hard to tell," Slade answered. "Think you'd know him if you see him again?"

"Uh-huh, I'd know him," Price said. "Come to think of it, he was a sort of ornery-looking specimen, shifty-eyed. I didn't think anything of it at the time, but now I remember."

Slade nodded and was silent.

They reached a point where Manuel Peralta's fence again turned west, dwindling away toward the far wall of the valley. Price regarded the rusty strands with a thoughtful eye.

"You know, Slade, I been thinking on what you said about wire and sheep," he remarked. "We've got hill pastures over to the west, too."

"No good for cows but okay for sheep," Slade smiled.

"That's right," admitted Price. "I sort of got a notion to sound out the Old Man a bit. He's set in his ways, but he's no fool and can see as far into a tree trunk as most. I'll bet you could talk him into digging some postholes and running in a few woolies. We don't none of us care over much for sheep, but you got to take in dinero if you want to keep a spread going, and the cow market has been a bit slow of late."

"Maybe I will have a talk with him later," Slade conceded.

"And I hope you decide to sign up with us," Price said. "We could use you."

"I'll think on that, too," Slade promised.

"Well, here's the forks," Price said a little later. "Going to ride to the house with us? It's getting late."

But Slade declined the invitation as he had declined that of Estaban Cartinas.

"I think I'll keep on riding for a spell," he said. "Feel like a night under the stars, and I want to get a look at the hill trail and Marlin."

"A pretty nice pueblo, Marlin," said Price. "We ride up there every now and then. Sort of lively, with the railroad, and more mines to the north.

Well, here's where we turn off. Be seeing you, feller."

The other hands said goodbye and Slade rode on, his eyes on the distant hills glowing many-colored in the last rays of the setting sun. They were really more than hills, being pretty close to being mountains, and they were rugged. Hole-in-the-wall country up there, he decided. Always was and doubtless always would be. Used to be a favorite hangout for the Apaches when they were lively in Texas, and still was for outlaws and smuggling bands. A wild land, but with a rugged beauty and the strength that is always part of the hills.

The sun sank and the mountain wall became somberly purple, tipped with pulsing fire. This also faded until all the world was gloomy and the clicking of Shadow's irons sounded loud in the deepening stillness. The trail, veering steadily to the left, entered the hills and ran between black rocks and twisted dark green firs and junipers. One by one the stars came out, glowing golden against the blue velvet of the sky. But not for long; the moon appeared to pale their ineffectual fires and throw a garment of silver over the rugged vista of slope and canyon and soaring cliff. An owl drifted past, its yellow eyes glinting in the moonlight. Flittering bats uttered their sharp, needle-like cries. In the distance sounded the lonely, beautiful plaint of a hunting wolf.

Slade rode on, experiencing the contentment that was always his when he was alone under the stars with only his horse and his thoughts for company.

But his thoughts kept him a bit too busy completely to enjoy the wild beauty of the night. For Yucca Valley posed a problem to tax the ingenuity even of El Halcon. That there had been a master mind directing the criminal operations of the section, Slade was convinced; but he had not the slightest notion who that elusive individual might be. Manuel Peralta had been a logical, almost a probable suspect, but the latest develop-ment had caused Slade to wonder if he hadn't been barking up the wrong tree. It seemed ridiculous that Peralta would foment a row between the Tumbling R outfit and his own riders. He would know that immediately many would conclude that he was back of the trouble, and all he'd gain would be more enemies than he appeared to have already. But somebody had tried hard to set the two outfits against each other.

Of course Peralta was not to be given a clean bill of health based on this particular develop-ment. His standing in the community was dubious, and Slade could not forget his apparent association with Curly Bill Elkins. Peralta still had to be considered.

But the fact remained that Peralta was, to an

extent at least, fading out. And if he was to be eliminated, who was to take his place? Slade hadn't the slightest notion. Of course he had been in the section too short a time to gain anything but the vaguest knowledge of its inhabitants, and the information he had been able to gather had come from biased sources. Well, he hoped to remedy that lack before long. Indeed, that was the real reason for his ride to Marlin. He wanted to ask some questions of somebody who would be conversant with the valley's affairs and its dwellers; questions he didn't care to ask Sheriff Blevins or anybody else in the valley. Any hope of getting answers from the sheriff would involve explanations he was not yet prepared to make. Sheriff Blevins appeared to be all right, but Slade did not credit him with better than average intelligence, and of his reputation for discretion, he knew nothing. And he didn't want his Ranger connections to become common knowledge, at least not yet.

"It's been my experience that bankers know how to keep their mouths shut," he told Shadow. "So we'll just try and have a little powwow with the big boss of the Marlin bank, who dispatched the payroll money to Chino on the stage that managed to get robbed."

Shadow snorted agreement, and Slade rode on. Until nearly midnight he rode, by which time he estimated he should be no great distance from

Marlin. The trail was now running through a shallow canyon and veering more to the west. A little farther on he saw a stream gleaming in the moonlight. Scattered thickets clothed its banks, and the ground was grass-grown.

Turning his mount, he rode to the creek, which was perhaps a quarter of a mile from the trail. As he anticipated, the thickets provided plenty of dry wood. At the edge of one which fronted the water, he removed Shadow's rig and turned him loose to graze. Then he quickly got a fire going and cooked an appetizing meal. After eating and cleaning up, he stretched out on his blanket and smoked a comfortable cigarette. He watched the stars for a while, but they soon grew hazy. With his saddle for a pillow, he turned over on his side and was almost instantly asleep.

Birds caroling in the thickets awakened Slade to a new day. Being in no hurry, he drowsed until the sun was fully up; then he arose and cooked and ate some breakfast. Shadow was refreshed by grass and water and appeared ready to travel. So Slade got the rig on him and rode on up the winding Yucca Trail.

For nearly two hours he rode at a moderate pace. Finally the trail left the hills, which were replaced by rolling ground. A little later Shadow's irons clattered on the floor boards of a wooden bridge that spanned a gulch about twenty feet deep with rocky sides and bottom, down the center of which flowed a swift stream.

Another half-hour of riding and Slade heard the wail of a locomotive's whistle and the pound of its exhaust. He passed through a wide grove, and the town of Marlin lay before him.

Marlin was about the same size as Chino but had more prominent buildings and gave the appearance of being older, especially the business district. Slade located the bank without difficulty. He looped the reins over a peg at a convenient hitching rack and entered the building. Approaching a clerk behind a grilled window, he requested an audience with the president, if he happened to be around.

The clerk hesitated, evidently decided he had better obey, and passed around the grill to a closed door on which he knocked. He entered, to reappear a moment later.

"Mr. Wetzel will see you, sir," he said, and led Slade to the door which he opened and closed behind him.

Hiram Wetzel, the president, proved to be a pleasant-looking middle-aged man with shrewd eyes. He nodded affably and invited Slade to a chair.

"And what can I do for you, young man?" he asked in a nicely modulated voice.

"I would like for you to answer a few questions, sir," Slade replied.

The president's eyes widened a little. "Well, within reason," he said.

Before speaking, Slade drew something from a cunningly concealed secret pocket in his broad leather belt and laid it on the executive's table desk. It was a gleaming silver star set on a silver circle, the feared and honored badge of the Texas Rangers.

The president stared at the symbol of law and order and justice for all, his eyes brightening.

"Oh, I see," he said. "You're here to investigate the robbery of the other day?"

"Among other things," Slade replied.

"I'll be glad to help in any way I can," said the president. "You wish to ask some questions?"

"Yes," said Slade. "First, was it common knowledge that the payroll money would be on the stage that day?"

The president shook his head. "It was certainly not supposed to be," he declared emphatically. "You see, we were robbed once before, some six months back, and since then have taken every possible precaution to safeguard the shipments. Which stage will carry the money is never given out for public consumption. Not even the driver or the guard know if there is money in the strongbox."

"Who does know?" Slade asked.

"Myself, the cashier and the bank directors," the president replied. "All men of unimpeachable character."

"It would appear somebody wasn't exactly unimpeachable," Slade commented dryly. "There must have been a leak."

"Unfortunately you are right," admitted the president. "In my opinion, somebody talked carelessly out of turn, with the wrong pair of ears listening."

"Possibly," Slade conceded. "How is it that the directors know when a shipment is to go out, instead of only yourself and the cashier?"

"Why, it was suggested at a meeting that it would be well for all to know the day, in case somebody might gather information that would make it advisable to change the date," the president replied.

"I see," Slade said. "And do you happen to recall just who made that suggestion?"

"Really I don't," Mr. Wetzel answered. "It came up in the course of a discussion, and I can't recall just who first advanced the proposal."

Slade nodded and was silent for a moment. "I suppose you have a list of the names of the directors?" he asked.

"Certainly," the other replied. "I can call them off from memory, for that matter, but I have them here on a letterhead."

He produced a sheet of paper and bent over it with Slade, calling off the names.

"The owner of the largest store in town," he explained; "the railroad division superintendent;

the minister of the Baptist Church; Clifton Worley, who owns the Monarch Mine to the north of here; Rance Rutledge, owner of the Tumbling R Ranch; Stephen Girton, owner of the Snake S Ranch, the biggest in Yucca Valley." He read several more names of Marlin businessmen, and paused.

"All except Rutledge and Girton are local residents, I gather," Slade interjected.

"That's right," nodded the president, "and you can readily see that these are not men who would knowingly pass on such information to anybody who shouldn't have it."

"Yet it would seem it was passed on to the wrong people somehow," Slade reminded him again.

"I'm afraid I can't argue the point," the president admitted ruefully.

"How about the gold clean-ups from the Chino mines?" Slade asked suddenly. "I suppose you handle those shipments and dispatch them to the assay office?"

"That's right," acceded Wetzel. "But there's no secrecy about those. They come via a light wagon with half a dozen armed guards riding attendance. Only a fool would make an attempt on those shipments."

"A fool or a real smart hellion who figures a way to outwit the guards," Slade qualified the statement.

"Is there anything else with which I can assist you?" asked the president.

"I guess not, unless you can call to mind somebody down in Yucca Valley who might bear a little investigation," Slade suggested.

"Well," said the other, "there's that man Elkins who Sheriff Blevins insists was an outlaw down in Mexico, although he doesn't seem to have been mixed up in anything since he moved here. And—" He paused, eyeing Slade.

"And Manuel Peralta?" Slade asked.

"I would hesitate to say such a thing about Peralta," the president answered. "He has always been a rather wild young man, a brawler and a trouble-maker, but I do not recall him ever being accused of anything really criminal. In fact, I don't remember hearing of any escapades on his part during the past couple of years. Perhaps he has settled down."

"Occasionally something does quiet down a young hellion, sometimes something surprising," Slade commented. He picked up his Ranger badge and stowed it away.

"I'd be pleased if you will forget seeing this, for the time being at least," he suggested.

"Certainly, certainly," Wetzel said. "I've already forgotten it."

Slade stood up, and they shook hands. "Good luck to you, Ranger," Wetzel said. "I certainly hope you are able to bring those scoundrels to justice. The payroll money was insured, of course, but that won't bring back that poor devil of a stage driver who was murdered."

"I'll do the best I can," Slade promised, and left the office. The bank president stared at the closed door.

"Well," he muttered aloud, "I wouldn't be in those robbers' shoes for all the wealth of Texas. Heavenly days! What a pair of eyes! They go through you like a greased knife!"

Chapter Nine

After leaving the bank, Slade hunted up a livery stable where Shadow could surround a helping of oats. He himself repaired to a restaurant and enjoyed a good meal. After that he retrieved his horse and headed back down Yucca Valley at a fast pace. He experienced considerable satisfaction, feeling that, in addition to quieting the row between the Tumbling R cowhands and the Boojer F *vaqueros*, the trip had accomplished something.

Slade rode steadily until he reached the point where the fork which led to the Tumbling R ranchhouse joined the main trail. He pulled up, hesitated a moment and then turned east; he was curious about old Rance Rutledge who owned the spread. Besides, it was nearly sunset and he would be late reaching Chino. At the ranchhouse, Texas hospitality would provide him with a meal and a bed more comfortable than a blanket spread on the ground. Presently he sighted the house, a big rambling structure set in a grove of pinions. As he drew near he saw somebody sitting on the wide veranda. It proved to be a girl, a rather small girl with big blue eyes and a wealth of curly brown hair. Not at all hard to look at, Slade decided as he pulled up in front of the veranda and bared his black head.

"Mr. Rutledge at home?" he asked.

The girl smiled and nodded. "Grandpa, there's somebody here to see you," she called.

"Bring him in, bring him in!" boomed a tremendous voice from within the ranchhouse. "Call a wrangler to take care of his critter."

Slade dismounted; the wrangler was introduced to Shadow and led him off. Slade followed the girl into the house. Seated in an easy chair was a little old man with a long white beard, a face that was a network of wrinkles and wonderfully bright and youthful eyes. His long hands were so thin that the light from a nearby lamp seemed to stream through them.

"So!" he said in his great voice which, coming from so frail and aged a man, seemed almost unnatural. "So! You must be the young squirt Walsh Price has been gabbing about of late. Can't talk of anything else. Sit down, sit down! Peggy, tell the cook to rattle his hocks. Cowhands are always hungry, especially young ones. Feeling lank as a gutted sparrow myself."

The girl giggled, slanted a decidedly approving glance at Slade and tripped lithely through an inner door.

"Come back here a minute," old Rance thundered. "I believe Walsh 'lowed this feller's name is Slade," he said when the girl reappeared, her eyes dancing and a dimple showing at the corner of her red mouth. "Slade, she's Peggy Fears, my granddaughter. Raised her from a yearlin'. Came home from school a couple of years back all growed up, and I ain't had any peace since."

Slade bowed with courtly grace over the little sun-golden hand she extended.

"My ride has certainly had a most pleasant ending, Miss Fears," he said.

"Call her Peggy, call her Peggy!" whooped old Rance. "What's your front handle, son—Walt? Good name. Peggy and Walt, that's it. I don't like stuck up folks, especially young ones. Get going, chick, and start that blasted cook sifting sand. Does he want us to tumble over from weakness?"

"I'll lend him a hand," Peggy promised. "It's really nice to know you—Walt." She flung another laughing glance over her shoulder as she departed for the kitchen again.

"Fine gal!" rumbled old Rance. "Well, well, Walsh Price says folks tell you're an owlhoot. Okay, one more won't matter in this blasted section."

He studied Slade a moment with his bright eyes, abruptly lowered his booming voice to little above a whisper.

"By the way," he said, "how'd you leave Jim McNelty?"

It was Slade's turn to stare. "How the devil did *you* catch on?" he demanded.

"Oh, I've known old Jim for years," Rutledge explained. "We used to ride together for the same outfit. Know how he works. Know the kind of men he picks. When Price told me about the things you've been doing and how you do 'em, I just put two and two together and made five instead of four. So Jim sent you over here to clean up the mess, eh? Got a notion you'll do it. Okay, the boys will drift in before long, so we'll just forget all about it for the time being and have another little gab later on. Reckon you may want to ask me a few questions about things in general. Been here quite a while, and not much I don't know about. Can give you the lowdown on folks here, anyhow. Here come the boys!"

The Tumbling R hands trooped in, Walsh Price in the lead. He gave a wild whoop when he saw Slade.

"So you got here!" he exclaimed. "Fine! Going to sign him on, Boss?"

"I don't know," replied Rutledge. "Would be so strange having somebody with brains around for a change, don't know whether I could take it. Go find out when we're going to eat."

Dinner in the big dining room was a hilarious affair. Slade sat next to Peggy Fears and found her a very charming companion. Walsh Price looked decidedly pleased when he glanced in their direction, and old Rance also appeared quite satisfied with the course of events.

After eating, the hands departed for the bunk-house.

"Got a little game lined up," Price told Slade. "If you'd care to join us—"

"Expect I will a little later," Slade accepted the invitation.

"Be looking for you," said Price, and followed the others.

Peggy was lending the cook a hand, and Slade and old Rance had the spacious living room to themselves.

"Good time to talk," said Rutledge. "Now what would you like to ask me?"

"First," Slade replied, "I'd like your opinion of Manuel Peralta."

"Always been a good deal of a hell raiser," replied Rutledge. "Used to gamble and drink quite a lot. Usually lost at cards, and redeye didn't improve his disposition. Can't say as I ever heard of him being mixed up in anything really bad. Sheriff Blevins has a mighty poor opinion of him, and I've a notion he thinks Manuel has a hand in the things that have been happening hereabouts of late. As to that, I don't know. Been quite a bit of change in Manuel for the past couple of years. Been giving most of his time to his spread and has been doing all right with it. By fencing his holding and bringing in sheep he got a lot of folks riled up, but I reckon Manuel just doesn't give a darn what folks think."

"He did only what the rest of you will eventually be forced to do," Slade interpolated. "Conditions are changing in Texas, in the whole West, for that matter, and there's no sense in being like the chick with the piece of eggshell on his back—'What I can't see I won't believe.' "

"You may have the right of it," Rutledge admitted. "I been doing some thinking along those lines myself, but it don't set well with most old-timers. They don't hanker for change."

"They'll accept it or find themself snowed under," Slade predicted a bit grimly.

Rutledge nodded. "Been a bit puzzled over the change in Manuel Peralta," he observed. "But maybe it was his grandfather getting killed that brought it about. They were always having rows till Manuel finally tore off on his own, but I've a notion he was really fond of the old man, down at the bottom. Funny thing about Sebastian Gomez, the way he got cashed in. He was just about the finest rider I ever knew; I wouldn't have believed there was a horse in Texas could have pitched him. But that's just what happened, according to Steve Girton and the couple of hands who went along on that trip to Jacinto, down in Mexico. He got pitched and busted his head. Maybe the poor jigger had a stroke or something. Steve Girton was mighty broke up about it. He always got along well with his grandfather. Steady young feller. Cold sort of fish, but nobody could say anything against his behavior. Always 'tends to business."

"Why do you call him a cold fish?" Slade asked.

"Well, maybe I shouldn't say it," replied Rutledge, "but that's the way he always strikes me. He drops in here quite frequent. I think he sort of likes Peg. Never seemed to have any bad habits, and he's all for efficiency and don't let sentiment stand in the way. After he came and got control of the Snake S—inherited from old Sebastian, you know; Sebastian's will left everything to him—he got rid of all Gomez' old hands who'd been with him for years. Steve said they were not good cowhands, and I reckon he was right; but it did seem a cold thing to do, to turn 'em out after all the years they'd been with the outfit. Guess he even fired the old cook who had been with Sebastian since he was a boy. Anyhow, the cook didn't come back from Mexico. Understand he had a son down there, though, and he might have decided to stay on with him.

"Manuel Peralta hired some of the old fellers, and they potter around. Manuel has a bunch of fine young Mexicans *vaqueros*, too, a salty lot, and they know their business. Understand you had a run-in with them yesterday, according to what Price said. I gave Price the devil over what happened, and I read the riot act to him and Ord and Perkins for jumping on that hand of Peralta's in town. Guess Peralta took care of that, after you'd stopped it. The three of them didn't look over happy when they got back to the ranch. Lucky you were in the Headlight when it happened. Price said you downed Peralta with one punch. Guess Manuel is still trying to figure what hit him. He ain't used to packing a licking, but I don't think he'll hold it against you. After he got to thinking things over he must have realized that you saved him from real trouble. He's got one heck of a temper. Quite different from his cousin, who never seems to paw sod."

Rutledge paused to fill his pipe with black tobacco. Slade sat silent, gazing at the blue spiral rising from his cigarette, a concentration furrow between his black brows.

Slade was developing a theory, based on his extensive experience with men and motives, and a chance remark dropped by Rutledge.

"Was Sebastian Gomez an active man for his years?" he asked suddenly.

"He sure was," replied Rutledge. "Can't say as I ever saw a more spry old jigger. Hopped around like a boy. But I guess he never had a sick day in his life, or a bad accident till the one that killed him. Yep, he could sure get up and hump. Handled his spread right up to the hilt, and if he hadn't always given away so much money I guess he'd have been a real rich man."

"Didn't leave Girton much ready cash, then?"

"Nope, but I guess Steve has been making the ranch pay since he took over. He spends a lot on trips over east and for new and improved stock."

Slade nodded thoughtfully and did not pursue the subject.

"I believe I'll drop over to the bunkhouse and join the poker game," he said a little later.

"Not a bad notion," replied Rutledge, "but you'll be in for a session. Tomorrow is pay day. The boys are getting the day off, of course, and can sleep late so they'll be all set for town tomorrow night. Pay day at the mines, too; Chino will be lively. Monthly clean-up for the mills, also, and it's a big one, I heard, close to ninety thousand dollars. The gold wagon will roll for Marlin some time tomorrow. You sleep in the first room at the head of the stairs to the right. I'll leave a light burning for you. Nope, I ain't going to set in the game tonight. An old jigger needs his rest. See you tomorrow, son, and we'll have another talk. Sleep as late as you want to. Peg will see that you get something to eat when you wake up."

The poker game lasted till the wee small hours, and Slade enjoyed the relaxation. Dawn was streaking the east with rose and gold when he returned to the ranchhouse. He lay down on the comfortable bed in the room at the head of the stairs, the window of which looked out on the ranchhouse yard, and was almost instantly asleep. And even as he was making ready for bed, the gold wagon rolled out of Chino, headed for Marlin and the bank more than thirty miles to the north.

Chapter Ten

The gold wagon, a light vehicle, was drawn by four sturdy horses. On the seat beside the driver sat an alert guard. Four more, armed with rifle and six-gun, rode two by two on either side. The wagon rolled north at a good pace, guards and driver chatting among themselves but keeping a wary eye on their surroundings.

Not that they really expected trouble of any kind; the wagon would be a tough nut to crack and it was highly unlikely that an outlaw band would chance the desperate battle certain to result if they attempted a raid on the treasure. It had never happened and they believed it never would happen. Just the same they took no chances, watching every grove and thicket and alert to every turn in the road, especially after they reached the hills, where the broad trail ran under beetling cliffs and around hairpin curves.

Guards and driver relaxed a bit when they left the broken country and the trail led across the open rangeland to the north of the hills.

"Chore almost done, and it's just about noon," one remarked. "Across the bridge and another couple of miles, and it's finished."

The wooden bridge that spanned the gully came into view. The banks of the gulch were covered with tall brush some distance to the east and west, but for a score of yards on either side of the span were free of growth.

The wheels rumbled on the floor boards, and the horses of the guards clicking along on either side. They were at almost the exact middle of the span when there was a sharp crack and a grinding of splintering wood. The bridge lurched, swayed, turned half over and crashed into the gulch, flinging wagon and horses into the swift stream or onto the rocks in one wild tangle.

The driver and three of the guards never moved after striking the ground, their bones broken and their skulls crushed by the terrific fall. The other two guards, who had landed in the stream, managed to free themselves from their struggling horses and, bruised and bleeding, began trying to climb the steep bank.

Out of the brush to the west rode eight masked men. Rifles blazed a volley. One of the guards fell back into the stream and his body was carried away by the current. The other lay half in and half out of the water, riddled by bullets.

The killers dismounted and swarmed down the bank to the overturned wagon. They hauled out the two strongboxes containing the gold, smashed them open with a sledge hammer. The ingots of precious metal were distributed and stowed in saddle pouches. Then the band mounted, after pausing long enough mercifully to shoot the crippled horses, and raced south on the Yucca Trail. The whole bloody episode had taken less than ten minutes.

Two hours later, a cowhand riding south discovered the wreck. He stared in horror, whirled his mount and tore back to town.

"The supporting timbers had been sawed nearly through," he told the crowd that gathered in answer to his yells and the banging of his six-gun. "Sure they were all dead, no doubt about that. The gold? I don't know. Maybe it's down there; maybe it ain't. I didn't climb into that crack to see."

Pandemonium and confusion followed. Belatedly, somebody thought to run to the bank and notify the officials there. The telegraph wires between Marlin and Chino hummed, but it was a good four hours after the time of the robbery before Sheriff Lake Blevins got a posse together and rode north. Another posse, made up of Marlin citizens, sped south.

Slade slept until nearly noon and awoke feeling greatly refreshed. He washed and dressed and descended the stairs to find Peggy Fears sitting in the living room.

"Hello," she greeted him. "I was beginning to wonder if you'd died up there. But the boys got up just a little while ago, so I figured you must have spent all night at cards."

"Guess that was about it." Slade nodded. "Had a good time."

"Men always have a good time at things that are forbidden women," she said, pouting prettily. "I guess they earn it, though. But come on; I waited to eat breakfast with you. Oh, I haven't been up so long myself. I read for quite a while last night, and the cook spoils me awfully; fixes me some-thing to eat at all hours. Come along."

Slade enjoyed a good breakfast with his charming table companion. Afterward, they returned to the living room where they sat and talked.

"Grandpa's out on the range somewhere," Peggy said. "He's always up at the crack of dawn. Goes to bed early, though. I hear a horse—maybe that's him now."

It wasn't. The new arrival who dismounted at the veranda steps was a tall, well formed and quite handsome man with a dark complexion and keen brown eyes. Slade instantly recognized him as Steve Girton, owner of the Snake S.

Peggy advanced to the door to greet the guest. "Come in, Steve," she invited. "Do you know Mr. Slade?"

"Mr. Slade and I met down on the trail the other day," Girton replied. "How are you, Mr. Slade? I guess you know I'm Steve Girton."

"So I understood," Slade said as they shook hands. "Sheriff Blevins mentioned your name, I believe."

"I was riding past and thought I'd drop in for a few minutes," Girton said. "How's your grandfather, Peggy?"

"He's all right; he's out on the range," the girl replied. "Won't you have something to eat, Steve?"

"I'd enjoy a cup of coffee," Girton admitted.

"I'll get it," she said, and left the room. Girton turned his gaze on Slade.

"Sorry you had a row with my cousin, Mr. Slade," he observed.

"Oh, just a slight misunderstanding," Slade replied lightly.

Girton shook his head. "I fear Manuel won't regard it in that light," he disagreed. "He always has a chip on his shoulder, and he's vindictive. He and our grandfather were always having words, until Grandfather finally washed his hands of him. And you had trouble with Bill Elkins, too. Look out for Elkins, Mr. Slade. He also is dangerous."

"Maybe," Slade conceded.

Peggy's arrival with the coffee put an end to the conversation. Girton drank it slowly, chatted a few more minutes and reached for his hat.

"Got to be getting on to town," he explained. "Today's pay day, and I want to keep an eye on my boys and see they don't celebrate unduly. Riding in for the bust, Mr. Slade?"

"I expect I will a little later," Slade admitted.

"May see you there, then," Girton said.

Peggy accompanied him to the door and then returned to her chair.

"A fine-looking man," Slade observed.

"Is he?" she replied indifferently. "I never really noticed."

"It would seem you are rather noncommittal where Mr. Girton is concerned," Slade commented with a smile.

"I am," she answered. "Steve's all right and I don't dislike him, but—" Her voice trailed off.

"And that sounds like there might be somebody else in the picture." Slade chuckled.

She colored prettily. "There is," she admitted. Abruptly her eyes met his.

"Walt," she said, "I feel like I want to tell somebody, and you're the kind of person who invites confidences. It's Manuel Peralta."

Slade's eyes widened. "The dickens it is!" he exclaimed.

"Yes," she answered. "We met a couple of years back, right after I returned from school. Of course I knew him before, but I was just a little girl then and I doubt if he gave me a second glance."

"But this time he gave you a third and a fourth." Slade smiled.

"I suppose so," she replied demurely.

"I begin to see why Peralta has eased up on his drinking and gambling for the past couple of years, as they say he has," Slade commented.

"Yes. He asked me to marry him, and I told him he would first have to stop acting in a way that would drive a girl crazy. He promised, and he's kept his promise."

"Wonder how your grandfather will take it," Slade remarked.

"Oh, I think I can manage Grandpa," she said. "He may paw sod a little, but I'm confident I can bring him around to my way of thinking. The boys will be horrified and so, I suppose, will our friends be."

"Not necessarily," Slade replied. Abruptly his face was grave. "Peggy," he said, "does Steve Girton know about this?"

"Why, I don't think so, although I can't say for sure," she answered. "He may have seen Manuel and me together sometime, but if he did, he's never mentioned it. I really wouldn't know. Why?"

"Was just wondering," Slade evaded a direct answer. He tried a shot in the dark.

"And Girton also wants to marry you?"

The dimple showed at the corner of her mouth. "Well, he did ask me once," she admitted. "I told him I just didn't feel that way about him. He said perhaps I'd change and that he'd wait."

"I see," Slade said thoughtfully. "Well, I've a

notion you and Manuel will make out okay. In fact, I feel sure of it."

The blue eyes were suddenly misty. "You make me feel good when you say that," she murmured. "You have a way of making folks believe what you say."

"Perhaps because I try to tell them the truth," Slade replied, his cold eyes suddenly all kindness.

Hoofs clattered outside, and a moment later old Rance entered the room.

"Well, suppose you're headed for town with the boys for a bust, eh?" he observed to Slade. "They're getting ready to ride. Come back soon; I want to have another talk with you."

Slade promised and rode off with the Tumbling R hands. They rode at a good pace, for the cowboys were anxious to get to town, and the miles rolled back under the hoofs of the horses. They passed Manuel Peralta's wire and sped on across the Snake S holding.

Lanky Tom Ord, who had an eye for horseflesh, kept exclaiming over Shadow. "Sure would like to fork him," he remarked at length.

"Why not?" Slade replied. "We'll switch for a spell." They pulled to a halt, and Slade dismounted.

"It's okay, Shadow," he told the big black as Ord approached him. He mounted Ord's bay, and they rode on.

"You can just feel power oozin' out of him," Ord enthused. "Bet he can sure sift sand."

Slade's eyes danced. His voice rang out:

"Trail, Shadow! Trail!"

Instantly the great horse shot forward, almost unseating Ord. Going like the wind, with Ord hanging on for dear life, he careened around a bend and out of sight. The Tumbling R hands shouted with laughter.

"He'll slow down when Ord tells him to," Slade said.

They rode on, chuckling. To the left was open range; on the right, a long, brush-grown slope rolled up to a rounded skyline. Around the slope the trail curved steadily.

"Say!" Walsh Price suddenly exclaimed. "That sounded like a gun."

Slade thought so, too, the whiplash crack of a distant rifle. His eyes were abruptly serious and he quickened the bay's pace a little.

They followed the slow curve of the bend; the view ahead was restricted to less than a score of yards. Then the trail straightened out a bit. Another moment and Walsh Price let out a yelp of consternation.

Standing by the side of the trail, his ears pricked forward, gazing up the slope, was Shadow. Tom Ord lay sprawled in the dust.

Chapter Eleven

Slade sent the bay surging forward, and he was the first to kneel beside Ord, who was breathing in stertorous gasps, his shirt front drenched with blood. Slade tore open the shirt and bared the wound. It was through the right breast and high up and was bleeding profusely.

"Get his shirt off, quick," Slade told the cursing cowboys. He ran to where Shadow stood and took a roll of bandage from his saddle pouch. Working with swift, deft fingers, he padded the wound to retard the bleeding and bound it tight.

"Bad," he said, "but maybe he'll pull through. We've got to get him to the doctor pronto. I'll have to carry him in my arms; any other way would probably kill him. Price, hold my stirrup. Hold it steady and don't let it slip. Okay, steady, now."

With the wounded man cradled in his arms, he inserted the toe of his boot in the stirrup. He tensed, his great muscles swelled, and he rose slowly and steadily until he was standing erect in the stirrup.

"Blazes! I wouldn't have believed there was a man in Texas who could do it!" Price sputtered as Slade swung his leg over Shadow's back and settled himself firmly in the saddle.

"Knot the reins and let them fall on his neck," he directed. "Shadow knee-guides. Let's go!"

He sent the black forward at a smooth running walk. His face was grim, his eyes filled with pain. Unwittingly, he had sent Tom Ord to what might well be his death.

For there was no doubt in Walt Slade's mind for whom the drygulcher's slug had been intended. Ord was fairly tall, and his hair was dark, and from a distance one tall man looks much like another; and there was no mistaking Shadow.

Slade rode sternly silent, but the Tumbling R hands cursed steadily and shook their fists at the brush-grown slope.

"Getting so nobody's safe in this infernal section," Walsh Price declared wrathfully. "Who in blazes would take a shot at poor old Tom? He never did nobody any harm."

"Just pure cussedness, I reckon," said Bounce Perkins. "No telling who'll be next. Sure wish Jim McNelty would send some Rangers here to clean out the snakes. Nobody else will be able to do it. The sheriff? He couldn't catch cold with both feet in a tub of ice water and a rainstorm running down his back!"

Slade also studied the slope, which soon would peter out. He concluded that a horseman sliding down the far side could circle around and reach the Yucca Trail south of Chino without being observed, unless some of the Snake S hands

113

working their range might spot him. However, with groves and thickets and swales a-plenty, he would very likely see them first and easily avoid detection.

Suddenly, from a grove a few hundred yards to the front, burst a band of horsemen riding at top speed.

"Now what?" barked Price, and drew his gun. A moment later Slade recognized Sheriff Blevins in the van.

Shouting questions, the two groups drew together and jostled to a halt. Blevins swore in weary disgust when the Tumbling R hands told him what had happened, and in a few terse sentences acquainted them with the details of the gold robbery and murders.

"And you haven't seen anybody on the way down?" he asked Slade. "Looks like we're riding a cold trail again."

"Looks that way," Slade agreed. "So long; we've got to get Ord to the doctor. See you when you get back."

Before they reached town, Ord regained consciousness, but Slade instantly forbade him to talk.

"Just one word," Ord whispered. "Is the horse okay?"

"He's packing both of us," Slade replied. "Now shut up."

Ord smiled faintly and obeyed.

They arrived at Chino and hurried to the

doctor's office, impatiently waving aside all the questions of the curious; the grim Tumbling R punchers blocked the office door and turned everybody away.

Doc Potter made a swift examination and nodded his approval. "Good work, son," he told Slade. "You've got the makings of a good surgeon in you, with those hands and no nerves at all. Quite likely he'd have bled to death if you hadn't patched him up pronto. As it is, he should be out looking for a chance to get hanged in a couple of weeks. All right; we'll put him to bed here for a few days where I can keep an eye on him. Then you can run a wagon down and pack him back to the spread."

Much relieved, Slade and the hands left the office to take part in the pay day celebration with easy minds. They found Chino seething over the gold robbery and murders, and their account of what happened to Ord didn't improve tempers any.

Tom Ord was popular, and after Walsh Price declared Doc Potter had 'lowed that Slade's swift and competent handling of the situation had saved Ord's life, men pressed around to shake hands with him.

After a couple of drinks in the Headlight, Walsh Price diffidently made a suggestion.

"Boys," he said, "I've a notion it would be a good idea to drop in a place a ways down the street, the Rosalita, where most of the Mexican miners and *vaqueros* hang out. Estaban Cartinas said he and his hands would be there tonight."

He glanced questioningly at Slade as he spoke. El Halcon nodded approval.

"Manuel will want to hear about poor Tom," observed Perkins. "Let's go!"

The Rosalita proved to be a big, softly lighted *cantina* with a wide dance floor and a good orchestra. Estaban Cartinas spotted them the moment they entered and whooped a greeting.

"*Amigos!*" he shouted. "Come and drink."

The Tumbling R punchers drank with miners and *vaqueros*, danced with the *señoritas* and generally had an uproarious time.

"You know," Walsh Price remarked speculatively, "I never before realized how much fun these places could be. The folks here know how to enjoy themselves. They ain't got much, but they know how to make the most of what they've got, and I reckon that's the important thing. They don't ask for the whole world on a platter and are satisfied with a saucerful of what they like. Guess that's the trouble with most of us—we ask for too much instead of scraping the dish of what we've got to the last crumb. Things don't have to be fancy to be nice."

"Uh-huh," said Bounce Perkins as he drained his glass, "and you can get just as drunk at a pine table as you can at a mahogany bar."

Slade chuckled. He, too, was thoroughly enjoying himself, and he experienced an intense satisfaction over the way things were working out. No matter what else happened, he felt that he was bringing understanding and tolerance to Yucca Valley.

Estaban Cartinas and the orchestra leader were in conference, the leader nodding emphatic agreement to some proposal Estaban was putting orth. A moment later the two of them walked over to the table where Slade and the Tumbling R hands sat. The orchestra leader carried a guitar.

"*Capitan*," said the Boojer F range boss, "it is said, and with truth, that you are the singingest man in Texas. Won't you favor us with a song?"

"Go to it, Slade; dish it out!" pleaded the cowboys.

With a smile, Slade rose and took the guitar. Tossing aside his hat, he walked to the dance floor.

"Quiet, please!" shouted Estaban. "*Amigos*, this will be a night to remember. Hush, and listen."

Slade smiled again, tuned the guitar to his liking and ran his fingers over the strings. Then he threw back his black head and sang, in a voice like the whispering of the breeze through the pines, sweet as the fragrance of the first flowers of spring, filled with the surge and thunder of Black Water River rushing through its sunken gorge, a rollicking old song of the range:

Roll along, little critters,
You're a-headin' for the train!
All set for goin' places,
And you won't come back again!
For the roundup days are over
And the cowboy's feelin' gay;
He's had his fill of workin'
And hankers for some play.

Yep, he craves a snort of red-eye,
And he aims to try his luck
At a-fillin' bobtailed flushes
And a-buckin' chuck-a-luck.
Roll along through the mesquite,
Dust a-foggin' to the sun!
For we aim to raise Old Harry
When the shippin' chore is done!

As the great golden baritone-bass pealed and soared under the low ceiling, the *cantina* was voiceless, all eyes fixed on the tall singer. And when the music ended in a crash of chords, a roar of applause shook the rafters, and "*Vivas!*" and "Give us another!"

"All right," Slade smiled, "I'll give you another, but first I want to play something for you, a little something I composed in honor of *Padre* Miguel Hidalgo Costilla, who first raised the voice of freedom in *Mejico*."

A murmur ran through the gathering at the

mention of the name of the martyred priest, the champion of the masses who had stood defiant in the face of the armed might of Imperial Spain and in life and death sowed the seeds that were to shoot and burgeon into the free Mexico of today. For who south of the Rio Grande but had heard the story of *Padre* Miguel, the friend of the lowly?

Adjusting the silken cord across his shoulders, Slade touched the strings, and under the hand of a master the simple instrument became a living thing that sang the joys and sorrows, the hopes and ambitions, the dreams and the star of victory of a people.

The music ceased in a breath of exquisite sound, and Walt Slade stood smiling at his listeners.

Again a roar of applause, and Estaban Cartinas' voice:

"Once again, *Capitan*, once again!"

So Slade sang them another song, a hauntingly beautiful song of the "land of tomorrow." And more than one hardened old-timer brushed his hand petulantly across his eyes and muttered something about the blasted smoke.

"Well," said Walsh Price as Slade returned the guitar to its owner, "I don't see why the devil he ever has to shoot anybody. All he needs to do is sing to 'em!"

After a while Price made another suggestion.

"Let's all go back to the Headlight and flabbergast folks a bit."

Flabbergast was the right word. The Headlight was used to sensations, particularly on pay day, but when the two outfits walked in together, men set down their glasses and stared. But as Walt Slade had already shrewdly surmised, where the Tumbling R led, Yucca Valley followed. Soon all was harmony and good fellowship.

"Sam," Kettlebelly Watson observed to his head bartender, "we're taught that the days of miracles are over, but I'm beginning to wonder. That big jigger they call El Halcon seems to have a way of dishin' 'em out."

"Aye, *patron*," said an old Mexican swamper who stood nearby with his bucket and mop. "Verily he is as our Blessed Lord in the days of old—he goes about doing good!"

"Pete," Kettlebelly replied soberly, "I believe you've got the right of it."

Price and the others were all for more liquid refreshment, but Slade hankered for some food. So he found an unoccupied table in a comparatively quiet corner and ordered a meal. While he was waiting for the order to be brought, a man entered and began searching the room with his eyes. It was Manuel Peralta, the Boojer F owner.

Peralta spotted Slade and made his way across the room to the Ranger's table.

"Mind if I sit down?" he asked.

"Not in the least," Slade replied. "Take a load off your feet and have something to eat."

"I believe I will," Peralta answered as he dropped into a chair. He beckoned a waiter and gave his order. Then for a long moment he gazed at Slade, his blue eyes speculative. He shook his tawny head and spoke.

"Slade," he said, "I believe that's your name—how the devil do you do it?"

"Do what?" El Halcon asked, a light of amusement in his own eyes.

"Make people do exactly as you want them to do, and like it?" Peralta replied.

Slade chuckled. "Perhaps because when I show them what I want them to do, it is really what *they* want to do, deep down, only they hadn't yet realized it," he answered.

Peralta looked contemplative. "Yes, that may be it," he acceded. "That may be it. Because what you want them to do is the right thing, I guess. But you sure have me guessing. The other night I was wondering how you were able to hit me like you did, with me looking straight at you and never seeing where your fist came from. When I heard about how you saved Pedro Garcia from getting roughed up by that Tumbling R bunch, I wondered how the devil you managed to do that without killing somebody. And after making Price and his bunch look like a pack of cub bears, you proceeded to make friends with them. And then you clean out Curly Bill Elkins and his hellions single-handed. Oh, I heard about that. Elkins himself told me. He's always tried to be nice to me, or appeared to. He stopped me on the street right after it happened. Then he sort of intimated that he and I both had a score to even up with you. I told him to go to blazes and left him."

Slade nodded. "I thought you and Elkins had had a mite of a disagreement, the way you walked off," he commented.

"Isn't anything you don't know, I guess." Peralta sighed. He seemed to hesitate, then arrived at a decision.

"I was riding up toward the Tumbling R ranchhouse before I came to town," he remarked casually.

"Yes?" Slade said with a smile.

"Yes," Peralta repeated, "and it seems you've taken Peggy in tow, too; she couldn't talk about anything else."

Slade shook with silent laughter, but was immediately grave again.

"I think, Manuel," he said, "that you and Peggy have put off getting married long enough."

Peralta looked decidedly startled. "Old Rance would hit the ceiling," he muttered.

"He'd come down again," Slade predicted cheerfully. "He might paw sod a bit, on general principles, but I venture to say Peggy can handle him. He'd end up saying yes. In fact, what you should do is ride right up to his *casa* and ask him for her."

Abruptly he let the full force of his steady gaze rest on Peralta's face.

"Only don't ride alone," he said. "Take two or three of your men with you. Don't ride alone anywhere for a while. Always have company. And keep your eyes open and a watch on your surroundings all the time. Otherwise Peggy may make a very pretty widow, and not enjoy it."

Peralta stared in bewilderment. "What the devil do you mean?" he demanded.

"I mean," Slade said quietly, "although I can't prove it yet, that in my opinion you're up against as cold a killer as ever came out of Texas, a man utterly vicious, without mercy and without conscience. If he learns how things stand between you and Peggy, and he may have learned already, he'll be out to get you, and he'll do it if you don't watch your step. Do what I tell you, and you may manage to stay alive for a while; don't, and you won't."

Manuel Peralta licked his suddenly dry lips. "Slade, I'll do as you say," he promised. "Blast it! You give me the creeps!"

"Hang onto the creeps and stay out of the ground," Slade advised.

Peralta looked at him doubtfully for a moment. "You don't mean Elkins?" he asked hesitantly.

"No, I don't mean Curly Bill Elkins," Slade replied. "Elkins is only a little wooly lamb compared to the man who tells him what to do and how to do it. Elkins is just a brush-popping owlhoot whose gun is for hire. That's all he is and all he ever will be, but he, too, is depraved and ruthless and will do the bidding of the man who is his boss. Now don't ask me any more questions. As I said, as yet I have no definite proof to back up my allegations. So I'm not naming names; but you'd better do as I tell you."

"I'm following your lead," Peralta said. "I'll jump through the hoop whichever way you say."

"Fine!" Slade replied. "Let's eat."

At the far end of the bar, Kettlebelly Watson shook his head despairingly.

"There he goes again," he mumbled to Sam. "Got Manuel Peralta eatin' out of his hand, and right after he nearly busted Manuel's neck for him. He's beyond me! Some folks say he's an owlhoot. Well, if that's so, I hope we get a lot more owlhoots of the same brand."

Walsh Price strolled over to the table. "Howdy, Manuel," he said. "Why don't you come over and join the party after you finish eating? Your boys are missing you. Come along."

Peralta drew a deep breath and glanced at Slade, whose eyes were dancing.

"Thanks, Walsh, I will," he accepted. "Be right over after another cup of coffee."

"And by the way," said Price, "I think the old man would like to have a little gab with you, about sheep."

"Sheep!" Peralta repeated.

"That's right," said Price. "He was talking to me this morning and figures our west hill pastures would be just as prime for sheep as yours and 'lowed you should be able to tip him off on some good buys in sheep and maybe tie onto some good herders for him. Drop around and see him."

Peralta breathed deeply again. "I'll do that," he promised.

"And don't put it off," Price said, and returned to the bar.

"Well," Slade chuckled, "it looks like you've got a good excuse for visiting the Tumbling R ranchhouse. Things seem to be working out."

"And I'll wager you had a hand in that, too," Peralta declared.

Slade smiled noncommittally.

The night wore on, with plenty of hilarity but no untoward incidents. The robbery and murders and the attempt on Tom Ord's life appeared to have had a certain sobering effect on the celebrants and were much discussed. Slade drank sparingly and listened to conversations and studied faces. He left the Headlight for a while and strolled about the town, dropping in at various places and looking over the crowds.

Nowhere, however, did he see certain faces he was looking for. It appeared that Curly Bill Elkins and his hands were not taking part in the pay day bust.

It was nearing morning when Sheriff Blevins got back to town, weary, disgusted and empty-handed.

"Not a sign of them or where they went," he told Slade. "A snake-blooded bunch of hellions for fair. They sawed the bridge timbers almost through, so that the weight of the wagon busted them and the whole shebang tumbled into the creek. Then they mowed down the guards that were still alive. Six men killed and ninety thousand dollars worth of gold gone. But how they got out of the valley is beyond me, if they did get out. I had the south pass guarded, and of course they couldn't have gone north. Begins to look like they have a hideaway somewhere. But where? We combed groves and thickets and gullies and didn't find hide or hair of them. They must have gotten out somehow, but where?"

Slade had a theory of his own and resolved to put it to the test without delay. He proceeded to get some sleep.

Chapter Twelve

It was late when Slade awoke. The sun was well past the zenith and he found himself ravenously hungry. To remedy that, he headed for the Headlight and some breakfast. He was eating when Walsh Price came in, bleary-eyed and considerably the worse for wear. He took one look at Slade's loaded plate and turned green.

"How do you do it?" he wailed. "I couldn't gnaw a hummingbird's drumstick. I feel awful."

"If you'd eaten more and drunk less last night you'd feel better," Slade told him.

"Easy to agree with you—this morning," Price grunted. "But next pay day I'll do the same thing."

"Sit down and have some coffee; it will do you good," Slade invited. "Then we'll drop over and see how Ord is making out."

They found Ord weak but chipper, and the doctor said he was starting on the mend.

"Don't suppose you know what happened, Tom?" Slade asked.

"All I can remember is something hit me a gosh-awful wallop and everything went black," Ord replied. "Next thing I knew you were packing me to town."

"Slug came from the ridge crest, I'd say, the way

it ranged downward," Slade observed thoughtfully. "Good shooting, all right."

"I'd like to line sights with the sidewinder," Walsh declared. "I'd show him what good shooting is. I'd fill him so full of holes he'd freeze to death from the wind whistling through them, the snake-blooded hydrophobia skunk!"

Price and the others departed for the ranch; Slade elected to remain in town.

"But I'll be seeing you soon," he promised.

It was long past midnight when Slade rode out of town, and most of Chino was asleep. He didn't ride to the Tumbling R ranchhouse, but south on the Yucca Trail. He rode for several miles, pulled up in the shadow of a thicket and made sure he was not being followed. He turned from the trail and headed across the Snake S rangeland, west by south, his goal the hills that, except for the pass through which the Yucca flowed, walled the valley. When he reached the start of the broken ground, he halted in a grove where a trickle of water ran, loosened the cinches and flipped the bit from Shadow's mouth so that the horse could drink and graze in comfort, and curled up under a tree to drowse till daylight.

When the sun was fully up, he began his quest, taking advantage of all possible cover and constantly scanning the distant ridges. He was confident that somewhere was a trail leading from the Snake S range into the hills and thence to the Yucca.

But as hour after hour passed without results, he began to wonder if his hunch was a straight one. The cliffs were sheer, the precipitous slopes impossible for a horse and rider, much less cattle. But he persisted doggedly, searching the terrain with eyes that missed nothing.

"I still believe I'm right, darn it," he told Shadow, who snorted with weary disgust and plodded on.

It was afternoon when he finally struck pay dirt. He discovered indubitable evidence that horses and cattle had passed this way no great time before. His pulses quickening, he began to follow the track left by the animals, which ran in the shadow of the south wall.

The task was not an easy one, for the ground was hard and rocky and cluttered with hampering brush. But an overturned boulder, the scrape of a horse's iron on a flat stone, a broken twig were enough for the keen and trail-wise eyes of El Halcon. On and on the trail led, with the west wall of the valley drawing near. And then, upon rounding a clump of growth, Slade saw a dark opening in the cliff face. At first he thought it a natural cave, but closer inspection proved it to be an old mine tunnel, quite likely driven by the enslaved Indians who had worked the Spanish mine in ancient days. And straight to the tunnel mouth ran the marks of passing horses and cows.

Slade pulled up and sat vigilantly alert. Did the

devils have a hangout in the old mine? It was not beyond the realm of probability. And if they happened to be in there now, he could expect a lively reception were he discovered.

But the dark hole in the cliff remained without sound or movement. He moved in a little closer, paused and again sat listening and peering. Shadow eyed the tunnel mouth unconcernedly and turned his attention elsewhere, which tended to reassure his master somewhat. Slade hesitated a little longer, then dismounted and stole forward on foot. He reached the yawning opening and halted. Still he could see nothing but blackness which remained utterly silent. No tang of wood smoke or other odor that might denote human occupancy came forth; only the dank air of underground passages. Slade turned and retraced his steps to where Shadow waited.

"Well, seeing as we've come this far, we might as well go the rest of the way and see what we can find," he told the horse. "But we'll need a light or we're liable to stumble over something and bust our necks. I believe I saw sotol growing a little way back, and dry sotol stalks make good torches."

He mounted and rode back to where he had noted the stand of yucca growth. Securing an armload of the dry stalks, he returned to the tunnel. He lit one, eyed the steady flame with approval and urged Shadow into the tunnel, the roof of which was high enough to enable him to ride in comfort.

Shadow's irons rang back echoes from the stony walls, but otherwise the silence remained unbroken, the blackness a steadily retreating barrier before the flicker of the torch. Soon they began passing side tunnels, but Slade elected to follow what was evidently the main gallery of the mine. His vigilance unrelaxed, he peered and listened, ready for instant action. But the tunnel stretched on with no signs of tenancy. Only now and then the proof that horses and cows had previously trodden its floor was apparent. Slade's interest increased and he experienced a growing excitement. No doubt but that he had hit on something.

But there was one disquieting element to the adventure: his store of torches was running low. The sotol burned well, giving off a satisfactory light, but it burned too darned fast.

For what seemed a very long time the gallery turned this way and that at random, doubtless to follow the veins of ore, but eventually it appeared to develop a more regular course, going south by east, it seemed, although it was hard to judge direction underground. Slade ruefully lighted his last torch and rode on.

All too swiftly the torch burned down until it was too short to hold. Shaking his head, Slade dropped the smoldering stump to the ground.

Instantly the darkness leaped at him like a living thing. Shadow snorted nervously but plodded on at a steady gait.

Slade lost all count of time. In the utter darkness, everything was deceptive. Time, distance and direction became elusive, for here there was no yardstick of contrast by which to measure them. The ever-present factors of normal existence under the sun were swallowed by an abyss of nothingness. Slade began to grow acutely uneasy; there appeared to be no end to this infernal coyote burrow. He experienced a disquieting suspicion that he might have turned into one of the side passages that led heaven only knew where. Also, if the gallery ended in a blank wall, which it very well might, he would be forced to retrace his way through darkness with no guarantee that he would turn right with so many opportunities to go wrong. Although the tunnel was cool, his palms grew slightly moist with clammy sweat. Shadow snorted from time to time, blew through flaring nostrils and shivered a little, which did not help. Shadow was not a nervous horse, but now he appeared to be growing apprehensive. Slade spoke to him in soothing tones, and he plodded on.

Then gradually the darkness seemed to lighten. At first Slade thought it was his senses playing him a trick, but soon he knew he was not mistaken; light was seeping through the blackness.

The gallery turned sharply, and ahead was a wide circle of brightness; it was the far mouth of the tunnel.

Slade heaved a sigh of relief; another moment and he rode from the dank burrow into the rose and gold of the low-lying sun. Glancing about, he found himself in a shallow valley that flowed northeast by southwest. Evidently the tunnel ran right through the mountain wall that hemmed in Yucca Valley. Doubtless it was one of the escape routes of which legend spoke, designed by the Spanish owners of the ancient mines against their hour of need.

Studying the valley, Slade decided that the Yucca Trail should lie somewhere to the east. A careful inspection of the ground, which was rather soft here, showed that horses and cows had passed not only to the east but also to the west through the brush-grown gorge, and the tracks leading west appeared to be the fresher.

Pulling up, Slade hesitated. He had found the outlaws' secret, all right, and the mystery of how they were able to slip stolen cows out of Yucca Valley was no longer a mystery. He made up his mind to ride west and endeavor to discover just where the trail running in that direction led, and to what. He spoke to Shadow, and the black horse moved slowly forward, Slade scanning every thicket and clump of brush, his ears attuned to any sound.

The sun sank lower, the shadows lengthened, and still the tracks of cows and horses wound on through the tall brush. Slade rode very slowly, for there was no knowing into what he might run at any moment. The outlaws were desperate men and would very likely give short shrift to anyone caught prowling their secret hangout, if there was a hangout and the valley didn't just lead to some other way through the hills.

Slade had ridden perhaps three miles when he heard a sound, the thin bleat of a steer, coming from a short distance ahead. He pulled up instantly and sat peering and listening, waiting for a repetition of the sound.

It came a moment later, but no nearer than at first. It looked as if the critter were grazing somewhere ahead, or perhaps were corraled. He rode on even more cautiously.

A little brook ran down the valley, prattling merrily over its stones. Slade glanced toward where it flowed unseen behind the tall brush and arrived at a decision.

"Shadow," he said, "from the sound, that critter isn't much farther on, and there's no telling what else might be ahead. If we go barging along with you kicking rocks, anybody who might happen to be there will hear us coming, sure as blazes. I'll just stow you away for a while and slide along on foot the rest of the way."

Turning the black, he forced him through the

brush until he reached the stream bank. In a little clear strip grass grew. Slade nodded with satisfaction.

"This should hold you till I come for you," he said. "And no singing songs to the evening star. Stay put till I get back."

Dismounting, he flipped the bit free and loosened the cinches, so the cayuse would be comfortable. Then, bestowing a pat on the glossy neck, he stole forward again, taking care to dislodge no boulder, to break no twig.

For a hundred yards or so, he forced his way through the growth, which gradually thinned. Pausing in a final straggle, he peered out from behind the leafy screen.

Ahead was a clearing covering an acre or more. About a hundred yards from where Slade crouched was a roughly built but stout corral, and behind the bars he could see a number of shaggy backs, fifty or sixty in all, he estimated.

But what interested him more was a small, weatherbeaten cabin that stood less than fifty yards from the edge of the growth. It looked old and had perhaps been built by some prospector or hunter years before. Now, however, it showed no signs of tenancy. No smoke rose from the stick-and-mud chimney, and the window which faced Slade was a dark and staring eye.

For long minutes he stood gazing at the building, searching for any sign of life, and saw none. No sound came to his ears other than the muffled grunting and mumbling of the cattle. To all appearances, save for its bovine occupants, the clearing was deserted.

This was not unnatural; the cows had food and water and would stay where they were until somebody came for them. Reassured by the continued lack of sound and movement, he left the shelter of the growth and crept cautiously toward the closed door. He reached it and stood listening. No sound came from within. He reached out and gave the door a shove. It swung open on creaking hinges. Slade hesitated a moment longer, then stepped forward and looked squarely into the muzzle of a gun.

"Get 'em up!" said a harsh voice.

Chapter Thirteen

Slade "got 'em up"; there was nothing else to do. Behind the gun was a squat broad shape and an evil-looking face.

The little eyes, hard as marbles and set deep in the fellow's square head, were extremely alert, and the hand which held the gun was rock steady. To make an overt move would be to commit suicide.

"Turn around," his captor said. Slade obeyed. A deft hand plucked his Colts from their sheaths, felt at the back of his neck and under his arms. With a grunt the fellow stepped back.

"All right; turn around again," he ordered. Slade did so.

"What's the notion?" he asked. "I wasn't going to steal anything. I just figured I might find something to eat in the shack; I'm hungry."

The other considered him with hard eyes. "Where'd you come from and how'd you get here?" he asked.

"Horse dumped me and went into the bush," Slade replied easily. "I figured to run him down, but he doesn't seem to be around here."

"I ain't seen no horse," the fellow replied suspiciously. Again he seemed to consider. Then abruptly he began to back away, his gun trained on the Ranger.

"Inside," he said. "Come ahead slow, and don't try anything—I got a itchy finger. Now, set down in that chair and put your hands on the table. That's right; stay right like you are and no tricks, or I'll shoot."

Keeping his eyes on his prisoner, he hauled a match from his pocket, fumbled the chimney off a bracket lamp, struck the match and touched the flame to the wick. He replaced the chimney, and a warm glow lighted up the room. In a swift glance Slade saw that there were staple provisions on shelves, wood stacked beside the fireplace and tumbled blankets on a bunk built against the wall. Evidently the cabin had known considerable occupancy. He eyed his captor.

"Well, what are you going to do with me?" he asked.

The fellow's brow knotted querulously as his slow mind pondered the question; Slade could almost see the wheels turning over jerkily. He watched the gun for a sign of wavering, prepared to take advantage of any opportunity, however slight, that might be offered.

None was. The man's brain might be slow, but his hands weren't, no doubt about that; there was no hesitancy in the way he kept the gun trained on his prisoner, the hammer at full cock.

"I'm going to keep you here till somebody tells

me what to do with you," he said. "Ain't nobody got any business snoopin' around up here. Some of the boys will be here tonight or in the morning, and if they figure you're all right, I reckon they'll let you go. If they don't—"

He didn't finish the sentence; there was no need to. Slade knew perfectly well what would be his fate if others of the outlaw band found him when they arrived at the cabin. The specimen before him was Border scum of a low order, set to keep watch on the cattle in the corral; he had proved his efficiency in handling the chore. Evidently he had sat in the unlighted cabin and watched Slade approach, all set and ready to take care of him when he opened the door.

"Uh-huh, I'll just keep you here," the fellow repeated. "Stand up and turn around. See that door over there? Open it and keep on walking. No tricks or I'll let daylight through you."

Slade moved to the door, which opened outward and was secured by a heavy bolt and hasp. He pushed back the bolt, pulled the door open and walked through. Instantly it was slammed shut and the bolt shot.

Slade found himself in a small room devoid of furnishings of any kind. Perhaps the cabin's original occupant had used it for a storeroom. He halted and drew a deep breath. He was seething with anger, chiefly directed at himself. He had walked into a trap like a dumb yearling. Absorbed in curiosity as to his discovery, he had relaxed his vigilance for a moment, with what might well be fatal results.

By the last fading light he examined his prison; the results were not satisfactory. The walls were of heavy logs mortised closely together, the floor of small split logs as hard as iron. The single window was too small for him to wriggle through, even if it hadn't been barred with stout wooden strips to keep out predatory animals.

He turned his attention to the door. It was constructed of thick planks that would resist a battering ram, which article he did not possess. There was a slight crack between the door and the inner jamb. He set his eye to it and could see his captor kindling a fire in the fireplace. With the blaze going, he began preparations to cook a meal. He had placed Slade's guns on the table, but for all the good they were likely to do the Ranger, they might as well have been in Mexico.

Slade turned his attention to the door again, the only possible avenue of escape. The hinges were on the outside, as was the bolt. The jambs were of stout timbers, squared and firmly set. The only break in the smooth surface of either was a large knothole in the outer jamb about in line with the bolt. Slade inserted a tentative finger in the hole and found it reached a little more than halfway through the squared timber, with a slight downward slope. On either side of the opening was a crack in the wood extending up and down for more than a foot. If he only had a bar or even a gun barrel, he might be able to wrench the wood apart; but he had neither.

The fellow had left him his tobacco, paper and matches, so he crossed to the far side of the room, sat down with his back to the wall and rolled a cigarette. He could hear his captor moving about, and presently a tantalizing smell of frying bacon seeped into the room.

"Hey!" he called. "How about something to eat for me? I'm hungry."

"Guess you can make out for a while," came the reply muffled by the door. "I ain't taking no chances with you; that door'll stay shut till the boys get here."

So that faint hope vanished; if the fellow could have been persuaded to open the door and hand in a plate of food, Slade felt he might have possibly caught him off balance for a moment and made a desperate bid for freedom.

His mind kept dwelling on that hole in the doorjamb; he had a vague feeling that it somehow offered a chance of escape. Pondering the problem, he absently fingered his cartridge belts, which the fellow had neglected to remove when he relieved him of his guns. He scratched one of the brass cartridges with his fingernail, turned it around and around in its loop.

Abruptly, inspiration came; the cartridges were filled with powder, and gunpowder, confined, explodes with great violence. He at once began making preparations.

Removing his broad neckerchief, he spread it on the floor beside him. With his strong teeth he wrenched the bullets from the cartridges and poured the powder onto the neckerchief, setting the empty shells against the wall with great care lest a tinkle might arouse the curiosity of his jailer. By the time he had emptied a beltful of cartridges, his jaws were sore but he had a sizable heap of the black grains; enough, he figured, nearly to fill the knothole. He felt sure that the explosion would so shatter the already split wood that the hasp would be loosened sufficiently to make it possible for him to smash open the door with his shoulder.

How to get the powder into the hole without spilling it? First he removed his boots so he would be able to move silently; then he unsnapped one holster and stole across the room to the door. As he expected, the small open end fitted snugly into the knothole. He retraced his steps and secured the neckerchief of powder. With the greatest care he sifted it into the holster and let it run smoothly into the hole. Removing the holster and snapping it back into place, he explored the knothole with a finger. It was more than three quarters full, plenty for his purpose, he felt sure.

The next problem was a fuse, but that posed no great difficulty. He tore off a long and broad strip of the neckerchief and laid it on the floor. A few minutes' work would prepare it for the firing.

And now the real problem arose: With the guard alert and wide awake, he could hardly hope to execute the maneuver successfully. But if he waited until he drowsed or lay down, there was always the chance that others of the band would arrive at the cabin. In that case his doom was sealed.

For a full minute or more, he considered the matter with an earnestness that amounted almost to mental agony, and at last came to the conclusion that the risk of immediate action was too great; he would have to wait in hope of a better opportunity.

It was long in coming, and Slade's nerves were keyed to the breaking point by the intolerable strain of apprehensive inaction. Through the crack in the door he watched the guard finish his meal, mouthing and chomping like an animal. He watched him light a cigarette and smoke it to a short butt. Next he cleaned up the dirty utensils, then slowly smoked another cigarette. Before it was finished, however, he was yawning, and once his head nodded almost to his breast. He muttered something in a low voice, pinched out the butt and stood up, stretching his long arms above his head. He looked around, grunted, cast a glance at the bolted door and shambled to the bunk. Without removing any of his garments, he lay down, drawing the blankets over him.

Slade still held off, although he was consumed by a fiery misery of impatience. Not until the guard began to snore did he move to complete his preparations. He rolled the strip of neckerchief into a wad and stuffed it in his mouth, holding it there until it was thoroughly damp. Then he emptied a few more cartridges and carefully rubbed the powder into the damp cloth to form a makeshift fuse such as is sometimes used on the rangeland to set off charges for blowing waterholes when nothing better is available.

With the fuse completed to his liking, working in utter silence, he stuffed it into the hole so as to wad the powder and yet in such a fashion as to ignite the charge. He knew he was taking one devil of a risk; should the fire race along the strip, as it would do if the mixture was not damp enough, he would very likely get blown apart along with the door jamb. That risk, however, he was forced to take.

Donning his boots, he tiptoed across to the door, listened a moment to his jailer's snoring, and struck a match. He touched the flame to the fuse. It caught with a quick sputter. Slade leaped back, covering his eyes with his hands.

There was a muffled boom, a rending and splintering; light streamed through the shattered jamb. Slade bounded forward and hit the door with his shoulder. It crashed open, and he was in the outer room.

The guard was coming out of his bunk, gun in hand. He fired wildly as Slade rushed him. Slade gasped and reeled from the shock as the bullet plowed a furrow along his ribs. He heard the click of the cocking hammer, but before the fellow could pull trigger a second time he had his wrist, bending it upward and back. The other's free hand shot out and fastened on his throat in a throttling grip. He slashed a blow at his jaw, but the guard ducked his face against the Ranger's breast and the blow landed on the top of his head, jarring Slade's arm to the shoulder but doing little damage.

Back and forth they reeled, locked in a death struggle. Over went the table in splintered ruin; a chair joined it and smashed to matchwood. They lurched and staggered on the wreckage, the guard endeavoring to bring his gun to bear, Slade forcing it back and up.

Slade's chest was bursting, and red flashes stormed before his eyes. He gulped and retched, trying to get air into his tortured lungs. He tore at the other's corded wrist, but the fellow grimly held on, panting curses, grunting and groaning.

Down came the gun muzzle, but in the nick of time Slade wrenched it aside. There was a booming report, and Slade felt something warm gush over his hand. The fellow gave a bubbling shriek and went limp, the gun clattering to the floor. Slade let go of his wrist and he thudded beside it, flopping grotesquely for a moment, stiffened and was still. He had obligingly shot himself through the throat.

Slade sagged against the wall, his chest heaving. His muscles felt like water and his head was spinning. In a few moments, however, his strength began to return. He lurched to where his guns lay amid the ruins of the table. With trembling hands he retrieved them, made sure they were loaded and thrust them into their sheaths. He straightened up, his still slightly befogged mind trying to decide his next move.

It was decided for him. He heard a sharp clicking sound, distant but steadily drawing nearer, the beat of fast hoofs on the hard cattle trail. He bounded to the door, flung it open and streaked across the clearing at a dead run. Before he reached the sheltering growth, three horsemen bulged into sight on the trail.

"Who the devil is that?" a voice shouted. "It ain't Crawley! Get him!"

A gun barked, and a bullet whined past Slade's face. He bent low and redoubled his efforts, weaving and ducking. Another shot came close. A third kicked up dirt at his feet. Then he was in the brush, tearing through it, butting into trees in the darkness, stumbling over roots. As he ran he whistled a loud, clear note. From ahead came an answering snort and a crash. Another moment and Shadow hove into view, blowing and whistling.

With frantic haste, Slade tightened the cinches, flipped the bit into place. He swung to the saddle and jerked his Winchester from the boot as the pursuers burst through into the clearing beside the stream. Slade flung the rifle to his shoulder and sent a stream of lead hissing toward them. A wailing curse echoed the reports.

"Trail, Shadow, trail!" he shouted.

The great black plunged forward. Slade fired again, twisting in the saddle. Replying shots spattered twigs into his face. Then Shadow tore through the straggle of brush and swerved into the cattle trail. Slade sheathed the Winchester and gave all his attention to riding. Bending low in the saddle, he sent Shadow scudding down the valley like a streak of darkness fleeing the sunlight. Another shot or two sounded, but the bullets did not come even close. Slade straightened up and spoke soothing words to the speeding horse. He had no fear of pursuit, barring accidents, but he was possessed of a great desire to get out of the devilish crack in the hills. No telling what else he might meet. He did not draw rein till the valley curved a little, and before him, less than a quarter of a mile distant, the broad gray ribbon of the Yucca Trail shimmered in the moonlight. He eased Shadow's pace and pulled to a halt on the dusty road. He estimated he was some three miles south of where the trail entered the pass to tumble down to the fertile soil of Yucca Valley.

Rolling and lighting a cigarette, he considered the situation. He had escaped from an exceedingly hot spot, he was frank to admit.

"Guess the devil or something takes care of his own," he told Shadow. "Sometimes I think I'm as shy of brains as a road runner is of scales!"

Yes, he had discovered the secret way out of Yucca Valley, but that, he expected, was about all. Before he could hope to get a posse together and get back to the cabin in the valley, the outlaws would either have removed the cattle from the corral or abandoned them. No chance to grab anybody, much less the head of the outfit. At any rate, he was pretty sure no more stolen cattle would be run from Yucca Valley via the old mine tunnel through the hills. Even if he hadn't been recognized by the three riders, it was very likely they'd figure out who he was. And even if they didn't, there would be little doubt in their minds but that somebody had discovered their hidden route and wouldn't risk using it again.

"So, feller, our hunch was a straight one, though for a time it looked like it might be just the reverse," he remarked to Shadow. "So we're going to play our luck strong, play another hunch. And this time it really *is* a hunch, or the shadow of one. Pure theory, nothing more, and based on just the shaky fact that we've been told *Don* Sebastian Gomez was a darn good rider. Let's go, horse!"

Slade rode north under the glowing stars. Threading the jaws of the pass, he saw the lights of Chino winking through the darkness; for Chino never slept.

Opposite the Snake S ranchhouse, which had been the home of *Don* Sebastian Gomez and was now occupied by Steve Girton, he pulled up for a moment and sat silently regarding the dark and gloomy structure. The huge building seemed to frown on the traveler, its unlighted windows like eyeless sockets that still could view, evaluate and assess. Houses reflect those who occupy them, he mused, and the old *casa* looked a fitting abode of darkness. He rode on, and less than an hour later, Shadow was comfortably stabled and his master was in the Headlight putting away a hearty meal. Afterwards he doctored the slight wound along his ribs and went to bed for a few hours.

Slade arose early and, after breakfast, rode south on the Yucca Trail. At the pass he pulled up and gazed back the way he had come. The gray track lay empty and, satisfied that he was not wearing a tail, he rode on at a fast pace.

Chapter Fourteen

But early as it was, his departure had been noted. The result was a meeting at the Snake S ranchhouse a few hours later.

"Why did that devil ride south?" Bill Elkins wanted to know. "Where's he headed for?"

"I'd be willing to wager he's headed for Jacinto down in Mexico," Steve Girton replied.

"But why?" Elkins repeated, accompanying the question with a string of oaths.

"That's a question I'd like to have answered," Girton replied grimly. "The man's a devil all right, and it looks like the bullet isn't run that can do for him. I was positive I had him the other day, up there on the trail, but it turned out I downed that blasted Tumbling R cowboy, Tom Ord. I still can't understand it. I spotted that infernal black horse easily, and I'd have swore Slade was forking him. And how did Carlos miss him with both barrels of a shotgun that night in the saloon? It doesn't make sense."

"Didn't make sense that Carlos would miss him with that knife a bit earlier the same evening," Elkins growled. "Carlos was the best knife thrower that ever came out of Mexico, but the hellion ducked it and then shot Carlos' gun out of his hand before he could line sights."

"Well, *you* had a little sample of how he works there in the Headlight," Girton observed dryly. "They say he's got the fastest gun hand in Texas, and I'm inclined to believe it. And what is worse, he's got a fast brain. I haven't felt right since he showed up here. And I understand he's taken my cousin in tow, to say nothing of his bunch of *vaqueros* and herders. Getting them and the Tumbling R hellions together is beyond my understanding, but he did."

"But what can he learn in Jacinto to cause us trouble?" asked Elkins.

"I don't see how he can learn anything," Girton replied. "But he's so blasted full of surprises, I'm worried."

"You figure he plans to cut himself a slice here?" growled Elkins.

"Maybe," Girton replied noncommittally, "but I'm beginning to wonder about that, too. I'm beginning to wonder if he might possibly be something other than what he's supposed to be."

"What?" demanded Elkins.

"Oh, he could be a Cattlemen's Association Rider, or a railroad detective," Girton answered. "Or he could be a Texas Ranger."

There was a stir among the dozen men gathered in the room, and a volley of curses.

"Girton, you can't mean that," protested Elkins. "El Halcon a Texas Ranger!"

151

Steve Girton shrugged his broad shoulders. "Well, he does things just like those devils do," he pointed out, "and since he's been here, he sure hasn't acted like the owlhoot he's supposed to be. I just can't help wondering."

"Well, a fast action gunslinger with El Halcon's reputation is bad enough," mumbled Elkins. "But a Texas Ranger! Steve, what the devil are we going to do?"

"There's just one thing to do; get rid of him," Girton replied quietly.

"But how? We sure haven't had any luck with him so far."

"I'll tell you," Girton replied. "Remember if he did ride to Jacinto, he'll be back. And he'll be back by way of the Yucca Trail; there isn't any other way. You know that trail, so here's how and where we will handle it. Crowd up close, you fellows, and don't do any loud talking. At a time like this even walls may have ears. That's an old threadbare saying, I know, but anything is liable to go where that infernal El Halcon is concerned. Listen, now, and remember we can't afford any slips. Slip this time and we'll all be done for."

He lowered his voice to little above a whisper. The hard-faced men clustered around him listened intently.

"It should work," said Elkins when Girton paused. "And I'll make it my business to see that it does."

The sentence of death having been passed on Walt Slade, the gathering broke up, the men leaving by twos and threes. Elkins himself did not leave until the rangeland was swathed in darkness.

In his big living room, Steve Girton lighted a cigar and chuckled grimly.

"Well, that should take care of El Halcon," he remarked aloud. "Next in line is Elkins and his stupid brush poppers. Then, with Peralta also taken care of, I'll be sitting pretty with nothing to worry about."

The cold killer puffed on his cigar and hummed a little tune.

All the long autumn day Walt Slade rode steadily, pausing only around noon to cook and eat. He reached the Crossing and forded the Rio Grande, which fortunately was low. Full dark had fallen when, dusty and travel-stained, he entered the little village of Jacinto, which had been the ancestral home of the Gomezes in the days of the Spanish king. He stabled his horse and repaired to the little office of the *alcalde*, the town's mayor. He was pleased to see a light burning within. Without the formality of knocking he pushed open the door.

Steve Girton and Curly Bill Elkins would have been even more disturbed could they have seen the warmth of Slade's reception by the mayor.

"El Halcon! Friend of the lowly!" he exclaimed,

starting to his feet. "*Capitan*! What brings you here? I am pleased, greatly pleased, and honored! Come with me to my home. The poor best I have to offer is yours."

Slade enjoyed a clean-up and an excellent dinner with the mayor. Over wine and *cigarillos*, he broached the reason for his long ride.

"*Don* Sebastian Gomez?" repeated the mayor. "*Si*, he lies buried in our little churchyard, where lie the bones of his father and his grandfather and others of the Gomezes. His was a sad homecoming, and it made all of us sad, although to us who reside here now he was but a name. His body came to the home of his ancestors, but his soul had departed. Thrown from his horse and his head broken across, said his grandson, *Don* Estevan Girton, and the two *vaqueros* who brought his remains. An old man, wrinkled of face, white of hair, but without a beard. Little to remind one, doubtless, of the fiery youth who departed to the great land to the north more than half a century ago to seek his fortune."

"Three men brought his body here, I believe you said," Slade remarked. "And his old cook?"

"There was no cook, at least to my knowing," said the mayor. "Only the three, who were very sad."

Slade smiled grimly. "You're sure about the cook?" he persisted.

"I am sure," the mayor declared. "Only the

three, and the body of *Don* Sebastian, which now lies in peace beneath the pines. May naught disturb it."

"Excellency," Slade said gently, "I come to disturb that peace."

The old mayor stared. "*Maledicto!*" he breathed. "*Capitan*, what mean you?"

"I disturb that peace that justice may be done and the wicked punished," Slade said sternly.

The mayor furtively crossed himself. "To disturb the last rest of the dead is a fearful thing, *Capitan*," he said. "But if El Halcon says it should be done, it shall be done. *Si*, I can obtain men who are to be trusted."

The wind sighed mournfully through the pines that drooped their needled branches over the grave which a simple headstone proclaimed was that of *Don* Sebastian Gomez. Patches of moonlight moved and altered shape as the branches waved, like restless souls emerging from the tombs to breathe the clean night air once more. The old church cast its black shadow athwart the grave and the figures that toiled by the light of carefully shaded lanterns. Two fearful peons plied mattock and spade under the direction of the *alcalde* and Walt Slade. Finally they uncovered the plain coffin, which was raised to the surface. The thick planks were still firm, and with difficulty the rusted screws were drawn, the lid of the coffin lifted and the pitiful remains of the occupant revealed.

The mayor shivered, and the peons crossed themselves and muttered prayers for the repose of the dead. Walt Slade bent low over the coffin and held the lantern close. He gazed earnestly at the skull, beneath which lay the long white hair of the dead man. Then he turned his attention to other portions of the skeleton, and his eyes began to glow.

"Look close," he told the mayor. "Look close, and forget not what you see. Note first that the temporal bone of the skull is shattered, as by a hard fall or a heavy blow."

"It is so," agreed the mayor.

"Now examine the left thigh bone," Slade prompted.

"Broken, I would say many years ago, and poorly mended," said the mayor.

"Leaving the left leg a trifle short, so that the man must have walked with a decided limp," Slade pointed out.

"It is even so," the mayor repeated.

Slade straightened up and gazed down at the skeleton.

"Excellency," he said quietly, "these are not the bones of Sebastian Gomez."

The mayor gasped; the peons looked very frightened. "But, *Capitan*," the former protested, "his grandson said the body was his."

"His grandson lied," Slade replied tersely.

"But if they are not the bones of *Don* Sebastian, whose are they?" the mayor asked.

"To the best of my belief, those of his old cook, whose leg was badly broken many years ago when he saved his master from the horns of an enraged steer," Slade replied. "Unless I was greatly misinformed, Sebastian Gomez had no broken bones. Also, I gather that Gomez was of pure Spanish blood, was he not?"

"Assuredly," replied the mayor. "The blood of Castile."

"While the cook, I understand, was part Yaqui. I'm not enough a student of Comparative Anatomy to say for sure, but the skull of this dead one does not look to me to be pure Caucasian. That could be definitely determined should occasion arise, but the broken thigh bone is enough, for the present at least."

"Then where is *Don* Sebastian?" asked the mayor.

"I wish I knew," Slade answered. "But although I have little on which to base it other than a hunch, I am of the opinion that Sebastian Gomez is still alive somewhere. If he had been killed, why would the killers substitute the body of the cook for his? That doesn't seem to make sense. Looks like Gomez somehow escaped them, or is being held captive somewhere, although the why of that last, should it be so, is beyond me.

But one fact is certain; before us lie the bones of a murdered man."

The lid of the coffin was replaced, the grave filled. The peons, sworn to secrecy and thoroughly frightened, departed, and the dead man was left in peace.

Slade spent the night with the mayor and rode north the following morning in a very thoughtful mood. There was no doubt in his mind but that the skeleton in the grave was that of Sebastian Gomez' cook and that the will leaving the Snake S to Steve Girton was a forgery; but proving it was another matter. He felt the case against Girton was not strong enough and that a good lawyer would very probably shoot it full of holes. Somehow, he hadn't the slightest notion how, he must trap Girton. He didn't know it, but Girton was due obligingly, although unwittingly, to lend him a hand in that difficult procedure.

Slade, still pondering the problem that confronted him, had reached the point where the trail ran along the edge of the canyon, with the cliffs soaring up on his right and the swift waters of the stream washing the rocky wall fifty feet below, when he was suddenly jolted from his abstraction by the sound of something singing past overhead. The whine of the slug was followed by the crack of a distant rifle. He twisted in the saddle and gazed back the way he had come. At a distance of perhaps a thousand yards, a number of riders were urging their horses up the trail at top speed. Puffs of smoke mushroomed from their ranks.

Slade surveyed them coolly for a moment, then turned back to the front.

"So! Looks like somebody wants to play tag with us, feller," he remarked to Shadow. "Well, if they're hankering for a game, they can get it. Trail!"

The great black shot forward, his irons drumming the rocky ground. Bullets continued to sing past, but the distance was much too great for anything like accurate shooting from the back of a speeding horse. Barring an unlikely mischance, there was scant danger of a hit being scored and Slade had every confidence in Shadow's ability quickly to leave the pursuit behind. Nevertheless, he was anxious to increase the distance between himself and the riflemen as quickly as possible. An accident *could* happen. He glanced back and noted with satisfaction that Shadow was fast drawing away from the group. He settled himself in the saddle and gave his attention to riding.

Shadow flashed around a bulge of cliff, and abruptly what had been little more than an exhilarating race became something deadly serious. Sitting their horses some four hundred yards to the front was a second group. Slade was not sure, but in one he thought he recognized Curly Bill Elkins. A chorus of yells arose as he came into view. Rifles cracked and bullets fanned past altogether too close for comfort. Slade whirled Shadow "on a dime" and scudded back around the bulge.

But now the riders in the rear were coming up fast, their bullets spatting the cliff or fanning his face with their lethal breath. On one side was the mountain wall, on the other the sheer drop to the hurrying black water below. Around the bulge sounded a drumming of fast hoofs. He was neatly trapped. From north and south the outlaws thundered in for the kill.

There was just one thing to do, one slender chance, a frightful gamble with death. Everything depended on the depth of the water washing the cliff base fifty feet below. He whirled Shadow again, to face the crumbling outer edge of the trail, and his voice rang out.

"Take it, Shadow, take it! You've done it before! Take it!"

Shadow took it, with a scream of protest. Far out over the lip of the trail he launched his great body, into empty air. Down he rushed, the wind of his passing streaming his glorious black mane upward like a flaunting banner. He struck the water with a mighty splash, and horse and rider vanished beneath the surface.

Down, down they went, until Slade thought they would never rise again. With a surging sense of relief he felt Shadow's irons strike bottom as he slid from the saddle. They began to rise, slowly. The current gripped them as with a mighty hand and hurled them downstream. Slade's lungs were bursting when they at last broke surface, rolling over and over. He gripped Shadow's mane with all his strength and grimly held on.

From the trail above sounded yells and a thunder-blast of shots. Bullets spatted the water all around the struggling pair; but the angle was not good for shooting at a moving object, and they were untouched. Another moment and they were forced to pass through another storm of lead as they flashed past the second group of riders and hurtled downstream at mill-race speed.

Instinctively Slade fought to reach the far bank; but he quickly realized he was only wasting his strength; the current was too strong to breast. His body was becoming numb from the bite of the icy water and he was gasping with effort. The shoreline flickered past in a dim blur.

The gorge began to bend. From almost due south it turned to a westerly direction and narrowed, narrowed until the black water washed the cliff base on either side with no encroaching strip of beach that might afford sanctuary. The stream roared hollowly between the towering walls that had greatly increased in height; and the current increased in power.

Slade could hear Shadow gasping and groaning. The black horse was in a bad way, numbed by the water's cold, battered by the surging current. His own great strength was nearly exhausted. Once he lost his grip on Shadow's mane and recovered it with a frantic grab as the heavier body of the horse forged ahead.

The canyon widened somewhat, to a breadth of perhaps two hundred yards, but still the water seethed against perpendicular stone walls on either side. Then abruptly it seemed to Slade that the current was losing its power somewhat. He strained his head up and peered forward. He essayed an exultant cry that came forth as an exhausted croak. Directly ahead was an island that split the stream in two. It was some sixty yards in width and of unknown length. Straight toward its shelving edge the current hurled horse and man. A moment more and Shadow's irons scraped bottom. Slade hauled himself up by the horse's mane until he gained a footing. Together they sloshed through the shallows, to sink utterly exhausted on a little strip of pebbly beach.

For a long time, man and horse lay motionless, breathing in hoarse gasps. The sun was high in the heavens, and its rays, pouring into the gorge, gradually warmed their numbed bodies and drew the chill from their bones. Finally Slade sat up rather shakily and gazed about.

The island was thickly wooded and he could hear birds calling amid the branches. An occasional rustling in the undergrowth hinted at the passage of some small animal. The cliffs that walled the canyon were towering; his eye grew dizzy in an effort to measure their height.

Gaining a little strength, he managed to draw off his boots and empty them of water. Removing his outer garments, he wrung them as dry as possible and spread them on the ground to allow the sun to complete the process. His guns and belts he placed beside them, confident that the well-greased cartridges had not been damaged by the submergence.

"May need 'em to shoot something to eat with, anyhow," he told Shadow. "For it looks like we may find ourselves holed up here for quite a spell. I'll try and figure a way out later—maybe."

Shadow got up enough spirit to roll a couple of times. He struggled to his feet, blowing prodigiously and gazed around, apparently little the worse for wear. Slade got the rig off him, and he ambled up the beach a little way and began to graze.

"Yep, we made it, but it was touch and go for a while," Slade said. "But we managed to pull through. Looks like a game trail through the brush over there. When you feel up to it, we'll see where it leads to. Looks like the coffee and other things in the pouches didn't get altogether spoiled, so when we find a good spot I'll join you in a snack."

When his gear had dried somewhat, Slade

cinched the saddle loosely, dropped the bridle over it and, walking a bit stiffly, with Shadow ambling along behind, followed the winding track that led into the thick brush. It straggled along for perhaps a couple of hundred yards and then entered a clearing walled by tall chaparral growth. Slade paused, staring in astonishment.

At the far side of the clearing, very neatly built of driftwood and branches, was a small hut with a crudely thatched roof. As he gazed, a man appeared in the doorway, a very old man with white hair hanging onto his shoulders and a long white beard. At sight of Slade, he uttered a great cry and hobbled forward, his wrinkled face shining with eagerness and joy. Slade stared, then abruptly laughed aloud. Dissembling his vast surprise, he took a long stride forward, holding out his hand.

"How are you, *Don* Sebastian?" he said.

Chapter Fifteen

The old man halted, amazement in his bright black eyes.

"*Señor!*" he faltered, his words coming haltingly, as from one who has not used his voice over a long period of time. "*Señor*, you know me!"

"Reckon I do," Slade chuckled. "*Don* Sebastian Gomez, is it not? I was hoping to run into you, although I rather feared I never would. Sure nice to find you squatting here like a wing-clipped duck. Will be interesting to learn how you got here."

The old man passed a shaking hand over his eyes. "I am bewildered, utterly bewildered," he said. "My brain swims. But it is so wonderful and so joyful to hear a voice once more. I had all but given up hope. *Ai*! so utterly wonderful.

"But come, *Señor*," he added with alacrity. "Come to my humble abode that I built with my own hands. There is a fire, and you can finish drying your damp garments. I have food to offer, too, such as it is."

"Fine!" Slade applauded. "And I've got coffee in my pouches. A little damp, but it should boil all right. Wouldn't be surprised if you would welcome a cup."

"It will be nectar fit for the gods!" *Don* Sebastian declared. "Come, *Señor*; later we will talk."

Soon portions of blue grouse were sizzling over the coals and coffee was bubbling in Slade's bucket. In a short while they sat down to eat.

"And now," Slade said as he rolled cigarettes from the papers and tobacco he had dried before the fire, "suppose you tell me how you managed to escape from Steve Girton and his two hellions."

Don Sebastian's eyes widened. "So you know of his perfidy!" he exclaimed.

"Yes, I know some," Slade replied. "I expect you can fill in the cracks for me."

"I had become suspicious of him," *Don* Sebastian said. "He always fawned over me, but for various reasons I became convinced that it was my property he valued rather than myself. He knew, of course, that I intended to divide my holdings between him and his cousin, with whom I often disagreed but whom nevertheless I loved and respected. However, I did not dream that he plotted my death until we began the journey to *Mejico*. Then I heard the two *vaqueros* who accompanied us—men I had recently hired at his behest—talking in the night. My ears are keen, and the old sleep little and lightly. I was frightened, as well I might be. When I was sure all were asleep, I stole away from the camp; but I was detected and pursued. One of the bullets they fired at me struck my horse. He fell over the cliff with me and into the stream. I was washed onto this island more dead than alive. The small bone of my leg was broken, but I managed to splint and bandage it and the bone knit, after a fashion, for old bones do not knit well. I had my revolver and some cartridges, and also matches in a tightly corked bottle that escaped breakage. So I was able to make a fire which I never allowed to go out."

Don Sebastian paused to drink some coffee with huge enjoyment and then resumed his story.

"There are small animals on the island and many birds," he continued. "I shot some and trapped others with snares. There are also berries, nuts and edible roots, so I managed to keep body and soul together. In my crippled state I dared not try to escape from the island, and I had little hope of rescue. I had almost despaired and reconciled myself to spending the remainder of my days on this lonely spot, like a second Robinson Crusoe, without the consolation of a man Friday. But now it would seem," he added with a chuckle, "I have one."

"But remember, Crusoe didn't spend his whole life on his island," Slade reminded him with a smile. "And I don't propose to spend all mine here, either. We'll figure a way to get off; discuss that later, after I've looked things over a bit."

Don Sebastian nodded happily. "And now, *Señor*, will you not tell me what strange fate brought you here to alleviate my loneliness?" he said.

Slade rolled cigarettes and then regaled Gomez with an account of the happenings in Yucca Valley. The old man swore a string of picturesque Spanish profanity, with a few impressive Texas cuss words thrown in for good measure.

"And he murdered my *amigo* to whom I owed my life, and set adrift my retainers, the friends of my youth, and robbed his cousin of his inheritance! The *ladrone*! May his soul burn in the fires of *infierno* for ever! *Señor*, if we manage to leave this place, there will be vengeance."

"Justice, rather," Slade corrected.

"And Manuel has settled down and will marry," observed *Don* Sebastian. "Good! Marriage and the responsibilities of marriage have a steadying effect on one; I know. He was always a roaring young blade, was Manuel, but his heart was warm. In his veins flows the hot, wild blood of the Gomezes, and in his energy and drive and independence he is more the Texan than the apathy and subservience of *Mejico*. Indeed, he reminds me much of what I myself was in my youth."

"I consider him a fine young fellow," Slade said. "Any man who can pack a licking and not hold a grudge has good in him. Manuel will do all right, if we can drop a loop on Girton and give him a chance to stay alive."

"We will confront that scoundrel and denounce

him for what he is," *Don* Sebastian declared.

"When the time is ripe," Slade said. "We must move cautiously. Girton is shrewd and resourceful and might figure a way to wriggle out of the loop if it isn't plenty tight. He seems to think of 'most everything. Substituting the body of the cook for yours was ingenious. He could have gone back to the valley with the report that you had fallen into the river and drowned and very likely gotten away with it. But he chose the safer way, and one more killing meant nothing to him. The death and burial certificate from the *alcalde* and *medico* of your old home town was convincing and naturally was not questioned. Improbable that anybody would call to mind the fact that nobody down there had ever seen you, with the possible exception of some old-timer who knew you when you were a young man and quite different in appearance."

"Poor Ralpho was much the same as myself in height and build, and one very old man looks much the same as another," said *Don* Sebastian. "And as you say, there would be little reason to suspect the story."

"And it also offered an explanation of the absence of the cook when they returned from Mexico," Slade added. "Oh, he doesn't miss many tricks, but he did miss one or two, as the owlhoot breed always do. He made a bad mistake when he tried to kill me there on the Yucca Trail and plugged poor Tom Ord instead. Nobody other than Girton knew I planned to ride to town that afternoon. Nobody but the Tumbling R bunch and Girton even knew I was at the ranchhouse. And he asked me if I planned to ride to town later. When I said I did, he holed up on top of the ridge and waited. If Ord and I hadn't changed horses on Ord's whim, he might have gotten away with it. As it was, it convinced me Girton was the man I wanted. Well, we'll see how things work out. Have some more coffee?"

The following morning, Slade considered ways and means of escaping from the island. There was plenty of driftwood and fallen tree trunks available, and after several days of hard toil with what assistance Gomez was able to give, he had an unwieldy raft constructed that he figured was strong enough to accommodate both of them and the horse.

"Doesn't look fancy, but I think it will hold together," he said. "If there happens to be a fall or a bad rapids down below, we'll very likely be goners; but it's the best we can do. Our only other choice is to stay here, which I don't particularly favor. Well, we're all set, and I guess we might as well get going."

Shadow, liking it not at all, was led to the middle of the raft and told to stay there. Slade and Gomez stood on opposite sides, each holding a long pole with which they strove to guide the awkward contrivance and keep it off the rocks.

Before the passage down the stream was negotiated, Slade was more than once convinced that the day of his death by drowning was at hand. The current was swift, the turns many and abrupt. The canyon had again narrowed and there was no beach on either side; just sheer walls of stone against which the water frothed and churned. Once they encountered a small rapids and were all but swamped and overturned. But finally the canyon walls fell back, the stream widened and shallowed, and they were able to beach the raft. Thoroughly worn out, they at once made camp for the night.

The following morning Slade tried as best he could to plot their position and concluded they were many miles west of the Yucca Trail. Shadow, however, was in excellent condition and offered no objection to carrying double.

All day long they threaded their way through gulches and canyons, over ridges and along the spines of towering hogbacks, until at last they saw the last rays of the setting sun shimmer on the broad gray ribbon of the Yucca.

Under cover of darkness they skirted Chino and made straight for the Tumbling R ranchhouse, arriving there well after midnight.

Soon, however, everybody was roused and exclaiming over what Slade had to tell them. The meeting between the two old friends, Rutledge and Gomez, was warm.

"Sure had given you up for a goner, you old pelican," said Rutledge, "but I reckon there's no getting rid of you. And if it wasn't bad enough to have to put up with one Gomez," he winked at Peggy, "we've got another of the same breed coming into the family. There ain't no justice!"

"You should be honored," *Don* Sebastian countered severely, "to receive one in whose veins flows the blood of Imperial Spain."

"Maybe," conceded old Rance, "but here he's just another ornery spread owner who raises sheep.

"Like me," he added with a chuckle. "Slade, I've got a big flock of woolies headed this way, and a passel of barbed wire. Come along, Sebastian. I got a bottle cached away, too; I figure we're due for a mite of celebrating."

With the greatest care, Slade laid his plans, for he suffered no illusions as to the calibre of the man against whom he was pitted.

"I'm counting heavily on Girton believing that I was drowned in the creek," he explained to the others. "I think he'll believe I really was, with me not showing up here. I'm of the opinion he'd figure that if I wasn't drowned, I'd show up again. I want to keep him thinking that way, so it's up to Gomez and myself to stay under cover. I also feel that, lulled into a false sense of security, he and Elkins and his bunch will get together to plan something. That's another mistake Girton made, tying up with Elkins and his crowd. Because of that, he has to keep on pulling jobs which perhaps he'd prefer not to get mixed up with. He has to in order to provide them with money and keep them quiet. Otherwise they are liable to get out of hand and do something on their own that will give the whole game away. Girton knows that and will have to string along with them, until he figures a way to get rid of Elkins and his men for good. I believe he is capable of doing it; a few more murders will mean nothing to him."

He paused a moment, then continued, "So I believe we've got a good chance to trap him and Elkins. It's logical to think they'll meet to do their planning at the Snake S ranchhouse. Seeing *Don* Sebastian and myself when we burst in on them should throw him off balance, especially *Don* Sebastian, who he is convinced is dead. So that's where we'll hit them. Our best place to hole up, I think, would be Manuel Peralta's ranchhouse. Manuel's *vaqueros*, who are good at that sort of thing, will keep a constant watch on the Snake S ranchhouse and report any gathering there. The Tumbling R hands will slip over to the Boojer F *casa* each night as soon as it gets dark, and we'll be all set to move when the word comes."

"How about the sheriff?" asked Rutledge. "Shouldn't he be notified of what's in the wind?"

Slade shook his head. "I'd like to," he replied,

"but it's too risky. I'm of the opinion that they keep close tabs on the sheriff at all times. Any move by him would be noted and the whole business would be given away. I'll deputize all of you, and that will give you all the authority you need."

The others nodded agreement. "Makes sense to me," observed Rutledge.

"*Don* Sebastian and I will spend the night here," Slade concluded, "but tomorrow evening we'll slip over to the Boojer F. I guess that takes care of everything. Oh yes, Rutledge, send somebody to notify Manuel that his grandfather is alive and well. If he walks in on him unannounced, Manuel will think he's seeing ghosts, and maybe have a stroke." He added with a chuckle, "Peggy, that should be a good chore for you."

Everything was carried out as planned. Manuel Peralta's joy at being reunited with his grandfather was profound.

"I've been blaming myself for your supposed death ever since I heard of it," he declared. "I shouldn't have gone off and left you like I did, although I hadn't the slightest notion that Steve intended to do you harm. What I've learned about him is a shock and an utter surprise to me. There won't be any more loco carrying on by me, that I can promise you; I've had my lesson."

So with all things properly taken care of, Slade sat back comfortably to wait until the time came to spring his trap.

Chapter Sixteen

Late and making up time, the Western Flyer roared through the night not many miles east of Marlin. Old Harry Frey, the engineer, bounced around on his lurching seat box, peered ahead through the rain-streaked front window, checked his air brakes and his water. He hooked the reverse bar up a notch, and widened the throttle a little. The racing locomotive increased its speed a bit. Frey leaned out the side window, ignoring the pelting rain, and squinted his eyes along the glistening twin ribbons of steel that provided the narrow margin between him and eternity. He ducked his head back in, wiped his glasses and swore. Again he glanced at the air pressure gauge, fiddled with the automatic brake handle. Everything was in perfect order for any emergency. Frey eased back on his cushioned seat with a grunt.

A red glare filled the cabin, and there was the musical clang of a shovel as the fireman flung open the fire box door and expertly scattered coal over the leaping flames of the raging furnace. Each lump of coal seemed fairly to explode under the intense heat. From the safety valve a squirrel tail of steam floated back steadily as the steam gauge needle quivered against the 200-pound pressure mark. Joe Grace, the fireman, knew how to feed a giant passenger "hog."

On boomed the great locomotive, exhaust pounding, side rods clanking, tall drive wheels spinning. The air vibrated to the thunder of the exhaust and the rhythmic crash of steel on steel. The long string of coaches glittered like jumbled stars as the light within streamed through the windows.

It was a wild night, with a mighty wind tossing the tree branches, the rain pelting down and thunder muttering overhead. Not a good night for railroading, especially with black cliffs towering on one side and overhanging the track. Rocks had been known to fall from their dizzy crests, and a rock on the track is one of the deadly hazards of mountain railroading.

But the Flyer was late, and in the chief dispatcher's office, miles to the west, a chattering telegraph receiver ticked off the passing of the C & P's crack train. The dispatcher jotted down figures on his chart as he checked the movements of west-bound freights ahead of the Flyer and east-bounds rolling toward it and sent the messages that would cause sliding switches to open and the more plebeian carriers to shunt out of her path.

The ever vigilant engineer checked his gauges again, peered out the window, glanced at the quivering steam pressure needle. He motioned to the fireman, and Joe Grace opened the left inspirator, sending a second stream of water pouring into the straining boiler.

Again a red glare filled the cab. Again a clanging shovel awoke the echoes. Grace, knowing that the inside of a curve would be on his side in a moment, slammed shut the door and leaped to his seat box. He leaned far out the window, blinking his eyes to free them of the fire glare, and peered ahead; he gave a frightened yell.

"Look out, Hank!" he bawled. "Wipe the gauge! Something on the track!"

Old Harry slammed the throttle shut and swung the air brake handle clear around. The thundering exhaust snapped off. The safety valve rose with a roar of escaping steam. Air screamed through the ports. The great locomotive bucked and lurched as the brake shoes ground against the tires. Back along the train, showers of sparks flew out on either side from the friction of clamping brakes. There was a clanging of couplers smashing together, a howl of protest from tortured metal. The locomotive slowed. Then the million pounds of wood and steel that was the long train surged forward to send the engine grinding and skittering ahead. With bulging eyes, Joe Grace stared at the huge mass of broken stone that blocked the track; it was rushing toward him with terrifying speed, the headlight beam flickering over its ragged bulk. Grace took one more look, leaped from the seat box and out the gangway. Poised on the lowest step, he strained outward, gauging the distance, tensing himself for a leap. Beside him, close, close, the black surface of the cliff flitted past.

Bang! Old Harry had hauled the reverse lever clear over. The stack howled as he jerked the throttle wide open. The drivers, working backward, screeched a protest and ground off great shavings of steel from the rails. The locomotive skated, slowed. Then again came an awful forward surge of the heavy train and the jarring clang of jamming couplers.

With throttle, air and bar, the old engineer fought to save his train, but it was a losing battle. Joe Grace jumped, slammed into the cliff and lay in a bloody huddle while the train ground past him. And with a rending crash the engine struck the mass of stone. Over it went, rolling down the steep embankment. Steam bellowed from a smashed cylinder, hot coals flew from the firebox, and the cab began to smolder.

Old Harry Frey, on his knees on the seat box when the locomotive went over, was hurled out the window. He struck a stunted pine, crackled through the branches and thudded to the ground to lie groaning and cursing. He was cut and battered but not seriously hurt.

The express car, next to the engine, was derailed and swung halfway around to teeter on the edge of the embankment. The other cars remained on the high iron. From them came the screams of bruised and frightened passengers who had been hurled to the aisles.

From the brush flanking the right-of-way darted masked men. They swarmed up the embankment toward the express car. A shot rang out, and one of the outlaws barked a curse. An answering volley smashed the express car window to splinters. Others sent bullets whining along the side of the train as a warning to the passengers not to come out. The bandits scattered as another shot came from the embattled express messenger.

A match flickered, there was a hissing sound. Something trailing a sputter of sparks hurtled through the air, struck the express car door and exploded with a roar. The door flew to pieces. A second stick of dynamite followed the first, to explode inside the car.

"Guess that'll hold the sidewinder," shouted a voice. The outlaws levered themselves through the opening and into the smoke-filled car. The shattered body of the messenger lay to one side. In a corner, bolted to the floor, a big iron safe stood with its door swung open, for a shipment stored in it was consigned to Marlin.

The robbers rushed to the safe and hauled forth stout canvas bags that gave out a musical clink.

In less than two minutes they cleaned the safe and leaped from the car, sending more warning shots along the side of the train, and vanished in the darkness of the brush. A moment later fast hoofs clicked into the west.

The outlaws rode swiftly for a mile or more, then halted beside one of the telegraph poles that marched sturdily beside the right-of-way. A man stood on his saddle, got his arms and legs around the pole and climbed it with ease. The sharp snip-snip of wire cutters sounded in the dark. He slid down the pole and regained his mount.

"That'll take care of 'em," chortled Curly Bill Elkins. "If they've got a telegraph instrument on the train, and they very likely have, when they try to cut in on the wire and send word to Marlin they'll get bad fooled. We'll be past the blasted town and on our way before they can get hep to what happened. Let's go!"

The murderous band circled Marlin and headed down the Yucca Trail. A couple of miles south of Marlin they paused again. Another pole was climbed and the wire cutters again brought into play.

"And now we're all set," said Elkins. "We'll be plumb in the clear before old Blevins learns anything, not that the old terrapin-brain is anything to worry about. And was this some haul! The best yet. Plenty of yellow boys in those sacks. How do you feel about it, Steve?"

"I'd feel better if I knew for sure that infernal El Halcon is dead," Girton returned moodily.

"What's eatin' you? Of course he's dead," scoffed Curly Bill. "Didn't he go over the cliff? Nothing can live in Black Water River."

"I suppose so," conceded Girton, "but I sure wish I'd had a chance to look at his dead face; the hellion has more lives than a cat."

"The fish took care of him," Elkins replied cheerfully.

Girton nodded. "Sift sand," he said. "We want to be holed up before daylight. If we meet anybody on the way, we'll kill him; we're leaving no witnesses."

Chapter Seventeen

It was Bounce Perkins, who had been to Chino scouting around, who brought the word of the outrage to the Boojer F ranchhouse.

"A thundering big haul," he concluded. "Nigh onto a hundred thousand dollars from the express car, shipments to the Marlin bank and the bank at Van Horn, and they killed the messenger—blew him to pieces with dynamite. Lake Blevins is a madman. He rode down to Curly Bill's place, but nobody was there. He's down at the south pass now, waiting. Says when the hellions show he's going to start shooting."

"He'll wait till doomsday," said Slade, whose face was set in granite lines. "But he can't fumble it any worse than I did. Oh, I was outsmarted, all right. They didn't meet at the Snake S ranchhouse as I was convinced they would. Must have had the raid planned and worked out for some time. Girton, a director of the Marlin bank, doubtless managed to learn when the train would be packing money. That's where I slipped again, I guess. I suppose I should have warned the bank officials against him, only the chances are they'd have thought I was crazy. And I was afraid if I took too many people into my confidence, somebody might talk out of turn and spoil everything."

"I'd say you were right," acceded Rance Rutledge. "Lots of folks just can't keep their mouths shut. But now what?"

"Last night was theirs, but tonight will be ours," Slade replied grimly. "I'm sure they'll hole up in the Snake S ranchhouse till things cool down. And they'll have the train robbery money there, too, which will cinch the case against them. We're riding as soon as it's dark and the rest of the Tumbling R boys get here."

Soon after dark the posse rode away from the Boojer F ranchhouse. The sky was slightly overcast, but the stars cast a wan glow that illuminated the rangeland with ghostly light. The weather, at least, was in their favor, Slade thought.

Slade rode in front, his eyes coldly gray. On his broad breast gleamed the star of the Rangers. Beside him rode *Don* Sebastian Gomez, grimly exultant over the vengeance to come.

With the greatest caution the posse approached the big ranchhouse, which stood dark and somber under the slightly overcast sky. *Don* Sebastian and Manuel Peralta, who of course were thoroughly familiar with the ground, guided them to a grove where the horses were left with a man to watch them. Then they stole forward on foot in the shadows of the old trees that shaded the building. *Don* Sebastian pointed to a gleam of light which seeped between closed shutters.

"The main living room, into which the door opens," he whispered. "There they will be. But look! They have a sentry pacing up and down in front of the veranda."

"And he must be gotten out of the way without noise," Slade whispered back. "There's nearly a score of desperate men in there, and if he manages to give the alarm they'll be ready for us and we'll pay heavily. I don't think they'll give up without a fight, but if we can break in on them unexpectedly, the element of surprise will be in our favor. Keep perfectly quiet and I'll see what I can make of that devil."

He waited a minute, studying the lay of the land, and then slid silently from cover and began inching his way through the tall grass toward the guard who paced slowly back and forth.

The intent watchers under the trees could barely follow Slade's slow progress by the faint radiance that seeped through the thin cloud blanket. They saw him reach the shelter of a small bush and crouch motionless as the sentry turned and walked directly toward him. The guard turned before reaching the bush, however, and Slade took advantage of his back to glide forward to the shelter of a second clump. Again he froze, a solider shadow in the shadow of the bush.

The sentry turned once more and retraced his steps. Less than three yards from the bush he paused, grounded the rifle he carried and leaned his folded arms on the muzzle, staring straight at the bristle of growth which sheltered the Ranger. To the perspiring watchers under the trees it seemed certain that he must perceive Slade's crouching form. For perhaps three minutes the tableau held, the sentry humming a little tune, the posse scarcely daring to breathe.

Abruptly the guard straightened, lifted his rifle. Walsh Price whipped his gun from its holster and trained it on the sentry, convinced that the crouched stalker had been detected. But the sentry turned in leisurely fashion and started to stroll back toward the porch. The quivering watchers saw Slade drew erect and take a long step forward, hands outstretched. He gave a bound; his hands closed around the watchman's neck with a mighty wrench. There was a stifled gulp, and the rifle thudded softly to the grass. A moment of convulsive twining of the two dark forms; then Slade slowly eased the flaccid body of the sentry to the ground.

"Busted his neck like a dry stick!" breathed Price. "Blazes! I'm shaking like a leaf in the wind!"

Slade straightened up and waved his hand; the posse crept from cover and joined him.

"Onto the porch and don't make a sound," he whispered. "Then altogether, hit the door with your shoulders, and every ounce of weight behind them. The door should give, even though it's locked and bolted; it had better!"

Noiseless as snakes, the posse mounted the steps and gathered on the porch. In the intense silence they could hear the sound of voices seeping through the door, and a musical clinking. Then, at a whispered word from Slade, they hit the door in a flying wedge, Slade the point.

The heavy door resisted the onslaught, creaked, groaned. Another mighty thrust and it flew open; the posse streamed into the room, which was occupied by more than a dozen men, mostly seated at a long table on which were bottles, glasses, and heaps of gold pieces. At the head of the table sat Steve Girton, Curly Bill Elkins beside him. Slade's voice rolled forth.

"In the name of the State of Texas, I arrest Steve Girton and others for robbery and murder!"

The outlaws stiffened, glancing sideways at their leader. Steve Girton didn't seem to hear Slade, even to see him. He was glaring with bulging, horror-filled eyes at the white-haired form of *Don* Sebastian Gomez. Foam flecked his lips; his face was writhed and contorted.

"You're dead!" he screamed. "Blast you, you're dead!" He leaped to his feet, pawing at his gun.

Slade drew and shot him between his staring eyes. His second shot knocked Curly Bill Elkins sprawling. The outlaws jerked their irons and fired wildly. The reports were drowned by the roar of the posse's guns.

Seconds later, Walt Slade dashed aside the blood that trickled down his fingers from a bullet-seared arm and gazed through the powder fog at the bodies strewing the floor and the five men backed against the wall screaming for mercy.

"Hold it!" he shouted. "They've had enough. Anybody badly hurt?"

"Nothing to speak of, I reckon," Rance Rutledge replied cheerfully. "Just a few nicks; they shot like a pack of school kids."

Don Sebastian Gomez gazed down at Steve Girton's dead face.

"My daughter's son!" he murmured sadly. "Bone of my bone, flesh of my flesh! May the All-merciful forgive his sins!"

Cowering under the guns of Manuel Peralta's bleak-faced *vaqueros*, the outlaws left alive talked freely and corroborated all that Slade had surmised.

"As I suspected, the two men Girton hired to murder his grandfather belonged to Elkins' outfit," Slade told Rutledge. "He brought them to the Snake S presumably as cowhands and chose them to accompany him and *Don* Sebastian when they planned the Mexican trip. That's how he got mixed up with Elkins. Curly Bill showed him there was an excellent opportunity in the valley to knock off 'easy' money. Girton was greedy for money and *Don* Sebastian didn't have much—gave most of it away—and while he had the

Snake S, an extremely valuable property, Girton wanted ready cash. He went on wild sprees over east, the prisoners told me. Posed as a rich cattleman and spent money like water. As you said, here he was a cold fish and a model of rectitude, but once he got away from his home community he really let himself go and gave his true nature free rein."

"And once he got mixed up with Elkins, he couldn't pull out," Rutledge observed shrewdly.

"That's right," Slade replied. "He couldn't cast Elkins off because Elkins had too much on him. The chances are he planned to get rid of Elkins, all right, by the murder route, but couldn't resist a couple more big paying jobs first. Yes, tying up with Elkins was one of his bad mistakes. He had brains and imagination and planned the jobs Elkins pulled, but he made the little slips the owlhoot brand always makes, and they were his downfall."

"Like bucking El Halcon," Rutledge chuckled.

"Rather becoming a bit too big for his boots and getting the Rangers interested," Slade corrected him smilingly. "If he'd stuck to cattle stealing and things like that, he might have gotten by for a long time, eventually disposed of Elkins and his bunch and ended up 'respectable.'

Well, he didn't, and instead ended up leaning against the hot end of a slug."

Under the guidance of Manuel Peralta, the house was searched and the gold ingots stolen from the Chino mine wagon were discovered.

"And it looks like here is the train robbery money, or most of it," Slade said. "Not so bad. We'll take these hellions to town and hand them over to the sheriff. If there are any more running around loose, they'll tell him where to find them. Here's your home back, *Don* Sebastian, only I guess you'll have to clean up this room a bit. Okay, boys, let's go!"

At the sheriff's office the prisoners were turned over to a deputy stationed there, who locked them securely in the cells. A rider was sent to recall Sheriff Blevins from his hopeless vigil at the south pass. The posse repaired to the Headlight for refreshment.

"He's still at it!" Kettlebelly Watson sighed to Sam, the head bartender. "Not satisfied with everything else, he turns an owlhoot into a Texas Ranger. Now I've seen everything!"

After a bit Slade strolled out of the saloon and stood in the street. Over the eastern hills the late moon hung red. Under its light, the Yucca Trail glowed softly. Shadow, standing by a nearby rack, craned his head toward his master and whickered softly. There was food in the saddle pouches, and it was a beautiful night.

Slade re-entered the Headlight and beckoned old Rance Rutledge to join him.

"I'm riding," he told the ranch owner. "My work is done, and Captain Jim will have something else lined up for me by the time I get back to the post. I'll meet Sheriff Blevins on the way and tell him all he needs to know; the confessions the prisoners made will take care of all the loose ends."

Old Rance watched him ride away, tall and graceful atop his great black horse. And back through the moonlight came the sound of his rich, sweet voice singing a love song of Old Spain.

Center Point Large Print
600 Brooks Road / PO Box 1
Thorndike, ME 04986-0001 USA

(207) 568-3717

US & Canada:
1 800 929-9108
www.centerpointlargeprint.com